# THE OLD PEOPLE

*The Old People*

THAMES RIVER PRESS
An imprint of Wimbledon Publishing Company Limited (WPC)
Another imprint of WPC is Anthem Press (www.anthempress.
com)
First published in the United Kingdom in 2014 by
THAMES RIVER PRESS
75–76 Blackfriars Road
London SE1 8HA

www.thamesriverpress.com

All the characters and events described in this novel are imaginary
and any similarity with real people or events is purely
coincidental.

A CIP record for this book is available from the British Library.

ISBN 978-1-78308-130-1

This title is also available as an ebook.

# THE OLD PEOPLE

ⓒ

A. J. PERRY

THAMES RIVER PRESS

For the old people

# THE KNOT

CB

This is how the Old People tie a knot: first, they dig a hole. To keep the knot from slipping or breaking, the hole should be dug in darkness just after the first big flood of the rainy month when the clouds are thick and the mud is thick and the night is dark enough for digging. Because knot makers cannot be hole diggers and hole diggers cannot be knot makers and because hole diggers dig holes at night while knot makers make knots by day, a knot maker with a knot to make cannot just dig his hole easily and be easily on his way. Just as any hole digger would know that knots tied by hole diggers do not make for holes that are very good the knot maker himself will know that a hole dug by a knot maker will not make for a knot that has been worth its making.

And so the knot maker does it like this. When the place for his hole has been marked and is ready to be dug the knot maker will look far away from the knot to the many things in the village that are not knots and here he will say without words that

4

there is a hole that needs digging. For this the knot maker might visit a friend to trade salt and here he will say to his friend, in passing, *If only there were a hole down by the field where the old umbilical tree leans out over the river*.... At this the two will do their trading and the knot maker will leave. But later when a friend has come by to trade salt the knot maker's friend will say what was said to him by the knot maker: that it would be good if there were a hole down by the field where the umbilical tree leans out heavily over the river. Again this friend will listen as if he has not heard the thing that is being asked for and only later while trading salt with an old friend of his own will he once again bring up the matter of the knot: *It will be good if the clouds come tonight*, he might say, *For a hole has yet to be dug in that place by the elderly river where the umbilical tree is leaning*.

Now these two friends can trade salt and when this is done the friend who has just listened to the talk of a hole will leave with his traded salt without ever learning of the need for a knot. But later while visiting with an old friend he too will make sure to point out what by now has been made clear over the countless generations that these friends have been trading salt: that there has yet to be any hole dug near the old umbilical tree that is leaning out over the river. Having traded salt for many years this friend will listen once again to the talk of holes that are not yet dug and of knots not yet made and later when he goes to visit an old friend he too will make sure to mention, in passing, that he has heard of a hole that needs digging and that the place marked for this digging can be found in the field where the old umbilical tree is leaning out over the river. In this way the need for a hole will go from one friend to the next until it at last reaches the man in the village who is best able to dig the hole that is being asked for: the hole digger. And when this latest mention of digging has at last reached him the digger of holes will gather his digging tool and make his way to the place by the river where the old tree is leaning and where the hole can now be dug.

On this island it has always been like this: knot makers making knots in the day and hole diggers digging holes at night. Of course before a hole can be dug—before a knot can be made—the place for the hole must first be marked. And so to mark a place for their holes the Old People drive a stake into the ground when the sun is at its peak and onto this stake they tie a marking knot to say that this staked place will be worthy of the digging. That night the sun will go down and the darker things of the island can begin. When the hole digger comes to dig—in darkness, never by light—he looks for the upright stake, then the knot, and then using his digging tool, he sets about his work. Here he digs slowly with care not to move any earth that does not need moving and when he is finished he takes the knot for himself—he will need it soon—and lays the stake over the dug hole so that it stretches from the side where the sun has gone down to the side where it will soon be coming up. In final darkness the nighttime digger of holes will go softly back to the place where he spends his days so that in the clarity of the next morning when the sun has indeed come up and the people of the village wake from their sleep to find the hole now dug, there will not be a person among them who can say for sure which of the island's hole diggers has just spent his night digging this hole—or for that matter whose hole it is that has just been dug. *This is a very good hole*, one of the day people will be likely to say while trading salt, *And should make for a fine knot someday.*

As always the digging tool that the hole digger uses to dig his hole will be a simple rod made from umbilical wood with a blunt tip at one end and a sharp tip at the other. The hole digger gets the wood from the village's wood carver in exchange for hard stones and fish and the special sacred salt that the islanders use for spiritual currency. He will have these things because he will have gotten them for his own work digging holes: the stones from the people of the quarry, the fish from the men who make their living as fishermen, and the salt from the salt given by the knot maker for the digging to be done. Because the Old People do not believe that a person who digs holes should carve wood, or that a person who carves wood should dig holes, when the hole digger sees that he needs a digging tool to be carved the first thing he does is to take the marking knot that has just been gathered from the end of the wooden stake and to add it to all the other knots that he has ever gathered after digging. Over time these knots will have been joined to each other to form a rope of tribute that is exactly as long as the hole digger's contribution to the art of hole digging. And because he knows that no request for a digging tool should be made using words that are spoken— which would be the worst kind of speaking—the hole digger will simply take his rope of gathered knots and coil it over his shoulder in the direction of the sun and on the darkest night of the month go with his coil to the tree where the wood carver is known to sit during the day with his carving. And there the hole digger will leave his knots for the wood carver to find. When the wood carver comes upon the hole digger's coiled rope the next morning he will uncoil it to full length and look over the chain of knots—each of them on its own and all of them as a whole—and in this way he will remember exactly who tied each knot, when it was tied, and for what purpose; by this the wood carver will weigh the value of these knots in his mind and if he sees that the hole digger is worthy of the tool that has been asked for he will know that a tool should be carved. And only then will he set about the carving of the wood.

To carve his wood the wood carver uses stone adzes that he gets from the adze maker over the course of many months; then comes the carving itself which takes many months more; and then there is the time—no less than three planting seasons—that the carved piece of wood must sit in silence before it can be given away. When the digging tool is finally ready and has been blessed by the island's seeing man the wood carver goes with his wooden tool to the icy waters of the river and there he sinks it deep into the cold mud where it will be left to age for forty generations. The waters will flow above this wood for forty generations and as he waits for these generations to pass the wood carver will go to a different place in the river where forty generations ago a fellow wood carver once sunk the same piece of wood into the cold mud of the river; and here he takes up the tool which is now as hard and as heavy as stone. His tool finally in hand, the wood carver says a short prayer for the birth of the tool and for the digging that will be done with it. Then he wraps the hole digger's coil of knots around the carved digging tool—round and round until the digging tool has been wrapped from top to bottom—and sets it under the tree in the exact place where the original request for a digging tool was once left by the hole digger. That night the wood carver will sleep knowing that his work is done, that it has been done well, and that in forty generations it will be unearthed by a fellow wood carver and given in the same way and with the same prayer to a nighttime digger of holes. In the morning the wood carver goes to the tree to see that the coil of knots and digging tool have been claimed by the hole digger during the night and to pick up the small offering of salt and the bundle of dried fish that the hole digger has left him as tribute to his work.

Of course to do all this the wood carver must first get the wood to be used for his carving. As an expert in the different woods of the island, the wood carver knows the location of every valuable tree or plant in and around his village. He knows where the largest and ripest umbilical trees have been planted for their hard wood purposes: as digging tools, as weapons, as stakes to be driven into the ground. And so when he needs more wood for his carving the first thing he does is consult with the village's seeing man who will tell him which of the many old trees of the island should be the next to be harvested. Because the Old People understand that although all people can carve wood not all people should be wood carvers—and, likewise, that all people are able to see though not all of them can be seers—the wood carver must trust the wisdom of the seeing man to see the things that cannot be seen, especially when it comes to cutting an umbilical tree. And though the wood carver himself cannot choose the tree to be cut—as this would be the farthest thing from seeing—he might make the suggestion, in passing, that, for example, he has heard of a certain tree that leans out over the river and that it is said to be very old and very hard and that maybe it is this tree that should be taken down. The seeing man will listen and on a day that is right for the purpose he will gather his things for seeing—his pebbles and his carved idols and his sacred knots—and he will make his way to the place by the side of the river where the umbilical tree is leaning. Once there he will arrange his things in the way that seeing men do and here he will begin to pray. Over the days that follow he will pray for the wisdom to tell one tree from the other; and for the assurance that the taking of this tree has not been done unjustly or before its time; and for the success of the cutting: that none of the men who do the felling shall find themselves beneath the branches of the falling tree; or be felled by it; or be weighted down by the heavy feeling that comes from having caused a great tree to fall. At this point in his prayer he will take the burden of the tree and place it on his shoulder in the form of a wooden idol. He will whip the branches against his own flesh using the knotty fibers of his sacred ropes. He will crush the smooth pebbles between his teeth, painfully, as if it were the grinding of hard wood against human bone. And when all of this is finished he will pause to wait for the signs that must follow: the windblown movements of the trees that only he can hear and that will tell him that it is this tree above all others, this very umbilical tree leaning out over the river, that should be felled for the sake of the knot maker's knot.

Over the next few months word will travel that an old tree is to be taken down and it is here that the rest of the village will come together to do its part: the knot makers will tie sturdy knots to bind the tree to itself and make ropes that can be used to guide the tree in the hurried moments when it is falling; the wood carvers will build tall stilts so that the tree cutters can cut away the highest branches at the tree's top. Finally, the people from the quarry will bring their stones and pile them one onto another to form a stone ramp stretching out into the shallow part of the river where the tree will soon fall. Everything is now ready for the felling and on the day when the seeing man says it is right the tree cutters will come with their cutting tools to chop at the tree's trunk. With expert swinging motions they will do this again and again, cutting deep into hard flesh until the sounds of falling can be heard. Because it is already leaning the falling tree will fall fast and the men below will shout and scramble and pull with their ropes. But this tree will fall only as far as the sloping ramp of stone that has been built beneath it. And here it will come to rest. For several long moments there will be an ancient silence as the Old People look at the tree on its crooked altar and think about what has just been done, what has just been taken away: the old tree—its limbs, its skin, all its bone and stone and heat—has just been taken away forever and given, forever, to the wood carver with his tool, to the hole digger with his hole, and to the knot maker with the knot that he is tying.

Here the seeing man will say a final prayer over a fistful of salt that he has scattered.

And then while the men from the village drag the wood down the slope of the stone ramp to the dryness of the river's bank where it will be cut up and cured and stored for the wood carver's use the wood carver himself will make sure to mention, in passing, that there is so much wood to be cut up and so many digging tools to make and so many weapons and so many wooden stakes and then, at the end of his speaking, he will add, *But before any of these things can be done it would be good to dig a hole near the place by the river where the old leaning tree has just been felled.* And his friend will listen. And this friend will pass on the request. And later when the request has been passed on and the salt has been traded and the location has been blessed and the hole has been dug and the stakes driven and the knots tied and the fish caught and the stones gathered and the prayers prayed and the adzes made—when all of this has been done—the wood carver will go to the hole that has just been dug in that place by the river and into its fresh soil he will set a young umbilical sapling to take the place of its felled ancestor.

In time the rains will come. And the sun will shine. The tiny sapling will become tall and hard and will grow into a tree that can be used to make the strongest and straightest digging tools and weapons and stakes to be driven into the ground. Once again the knot maker will go to the place by the river where the umbilical tree is leaning and here he will stand with his rope to give thanks. For the tree. For the knot. For the hole that will be dug. For the tool that has been carved. And when this is done he will begin tying the knot without which no tree can be made to fall—the final knot that will tell the tree cutters to begin their cutting. Over the next few days, while the tree cutters are readying their cutting tools and the people of the quarry are bringing the stones to build their ramp and the seeing man is sitting on the ground with his many things of prayer—while all of this is happening— the knot maker will stand to the side tying the umbilical tree's knot of passage, the knot that will mark the journey of the tree from this life to the other. And as the knot maker works to make this knot, his hands looping and tucking the knot into shape, the crowd will avert its eyes. The men with the ropes will lean back into their ropes ready to guide the tree to the ground once it has begun to fall. And the men with the tree cutting tools, their cutting tools raised high over their heads, will eye the hard neck of the leaning tree waiting for the exact moment when the knot maker has finished his knot so that their cutting can begin.


Back in the village the women of the island will be following all of this from a distance. As the Old People do not believe that a man should do the things that women do—or that a woman should do the things that men do—the women of the island do not dig holes or carve wood or catch fish or gather stones. They do not say prayers or tie knots. They do not cut trees or make adzes but instead contribute to the knot maker's knot in other ways. When the men have returned from the river where the old umbilical tree has just been felled the women will greet them and share fish with them and soothe their muscles and dress their wounds and listen to their stories of falling branches; later, when the fires of their homes have burnt down, these women will open their wombs to the briny waters that stream forth. In time they will turn this brine into young boys who will one day learn to carve wood and catch fish and fell trees. And they will turn these waters into the young girls who will soothe muscles and dress wounds and who will one day take into themselves the many streams of brine that pour out. When a woman learns that the generations will be flowing through her and that she will soon be giving birth to a child the first thing she does is to mention to her husband, in passing, that he might want to start digging a hole. This hole to be dug will be the source of much joy in the village, and so the next day the man will mention to a friend, in passing, that a hole might very well be dug over by the salt beds where the salt makers make their salt. The friend will pass along the word and the word will be passed along and in this way the Old People will dig this hole over many fertile months, friends trading salt for salt and words unspoken for words unheard, until the digging at last reaches the island's digger of holes who now takes up the wood carver's digging tool to dig this hole.

When the carrying woman finally gives birth to the child the first person she sees, apart from the midwife with her basket of birth residue, is the knot maker himself who carefully ties up the skin of the child's navel with the knot that separates this life from the other. It is the most basic of all knots and after tying it the knot maker will leave and the seeing man will come with his things for seeing—his pebbles and his carved idols and his sacred knots—and he will say a prayer for the upcoming journey of the child: that the child should grow to be strong and healthy and wise in the ways of indirectness; that he will be skilled in the art of adze making or wood carving or fish catching; or, if the child is a girl, that she will be able to take the brine of her fathers and do with it what has been done without fail by the women who came before her. Once again many fistfuls of salt will be scattered to consecrate the coming of the child. When the seeing man has finished his ceremony the child's father will take the blood of this birth to the hole that has been dug near the place by the ocean where the salt makers make their salt. Into this expertly dug hole he will place his offering: the blood, some salt, a female shadow fish, and the tiny seed of a kwa plant to mark the birth. If the child is a boy the boy's father will then go to the place where his family's ancestral rope of knots is hidden in the cool and quiet darkness of the caves and here, in darkness, the father will trace along the length of the rope until he finds his own knot and onto the knot once tied by his own father when he was born he will tie the knot of his son. If the child is a girl the girl's mother will do the same, going when she is ready to the secret cave where the elaborate rope of her mother's ancestry is kept and, in darkness, adding the knot to her own knot which a generation ago was tied by her mother when she was born. Although the Old People do not believe that knots should be tied by people who are not knot makers, or that people who are not knot makers should tie knots, this type of knot, the knot of ancestry and descent, is the only type that can be tied from beginning to end by a person who is not a maker of knots: to hide their genealogies from the sunlight the Old People must do it like this. And so it is that this knot is the only one that most fathers will have the occasion to tie; and it is the only knot that a woman will ever tie such that if a woman has three daughters in her lifetime it can be said, without fail, that during her lifetime she has tied exactly three knots.

After the blood has been buried and the genealogy preserved the storytellers will go from house to house with their firemaking tools—the curved bow and the fire sticks and the rope that is used to spin them into each other—to light the morning fires of the village. Traveling with their firemaking tools, and with stories of the child now born, the storytellers will pass the many morning time activities of the village: the people of the quarry piling their stones into large stone piles; the tree cutters cutting away the branches from the old umbilical tree that is leaning out over the river and that will soon be cut down; the men who make their living as fishermen loading their fishing nets into their boats. As they walk with their smoldering tools the storytellers will see the wood carvers carving wood and adze makers making adzes; knot makers tying their knots in the shade of the village's original knotmaking tree and the seers of the island sitting for days at a time on the stony ground of prayer. Just as no two flames are ever the same, storytellers themselves do not travel in groups but prefer instead to take their own paths around the island. And so when a storyteller has reached the other side of the village he will bend down to make his fire, squatting over his firemaking tools and using his rope to spin one wood stick into another until the place where these sticks meet becomes as hot as fire itself. By now the people of the village will have circled around the storyteller waiting for the flame to take shape and for the stories that will follow. To the rhythm of rope and stick, of one piece of wood being spun into another, the Old People will trade the stories of their day: the people of the quarry will tell the storyteller about all that is happening in the quarry; the salt makers about the salt that is being made; and the women of the island about the many things taking place in their houses and in their bellies and in the cool caves where the ropes of their ancestry are kept. The storyteller will listen to all these things and when he has heard the stories of this place he will tell his own stories which have been told to him by the other people of the island. As thin wisps of smoke begin to rise from the wood being spun the squatting storyteller will tell about the men who make their living as fishermen, who have just returned with a net full of the choicest shadow fish; and about the young tree cutter whose fall from a tree while doing his cutting is now a subject of great unease; and about the seeing man who for some time now has been sitting beside the old umbilical tree that still leans out over the river. The storyteller will tell all this, faithfully, until the first real flames begin to glow out from under his fingers. At this a sudden hush will fall upon the circle. Because it is not a good thing for words and fire to mix too closely and because the Old People have more respect for fire than they do for words—though more fear of words than fire—the people of the village will keep a reverent silence when standing anywhere near a flame that is burning outright. This silence will last until the fire dies down to ember and the silence turns to ash. And when the morning fire has finally been made and the stories of this morning have been traded and the genealogies preserved the storyteller will gather up his firemaking tools and with his tools in hand move on to other parts of the island, to the many places of the village where the Old People are still waiting for the heat that comes from the fire of the storyteller's fires and for the light that comes from his words.

And all the while the trees of the island will shake and rustle in the wind. The sun rises and falls. The ocean crawls up to the shores of the beach where the men who make their living as fishermen will one day leave their fishing boats. And then it crawls back out. In the bubbling foam of the breaking wave a sand crab has just taken a smaller crab in its jaws and is now tucking itself back down into the sand. It has been morning for some time and the land is silent. The air is still. In the darkness that comes before storytelling the clouds move across the sky and the winds of the island blow back and forth, first one way then the other. At last the sun begins to rise over the place on the beach where the men who make their living as fishermen have decided to keep their boats. The earth accepts the heat. The plants spread out. The umbilical tree down by the river becomes taller and harder and eventually begins to lean out over the river. The rains fall in the mountains and make their way to the sea, to the place where the men with the fishing boats have decided to make their living as fishermen. The rain flows from the top of the mountain to the bottom of the sea, the generations pass slowly, a river is formed to connect them, and the digging tools that have been left in the icy waters of the river become as hard and as heavy as stone. The men in the boats catch many fish. The wood carvers learn to carve wood. The storytellers learn to make fire. In time the generations flow from one to the other like brine into mud. Dirt is kicked onto the embers.

The knots of ancestry and descent lie quietly in the cool darkness of the caves. The sun falls again. Small knots are tied to the driven stakes and the holes of the island are marked for digging. Once again there will be comfort of darkness and in this darkness the hole diggers will soon be coming out to do their work.

೫

And then one day it happens. The knot maker, while walking through the field by the river where the old umbilical tree is leaning, looks down to see the fresh heap of soil that means his hole has finally been dug: the hole digger has done his work. At this the knot maker will be grateful because now at last he can continue the making of his knot by placing a tiny seed into the hole and covering it with soil. The knot maker places the seed into the hole and covers it and waits patiently for the plant to take shape. It takes many years for a kwa plant to take its full shape, and so with little else to do the knot maker walks back to his village and in the cool shade of the village's original knotmaking tree devotes his time to studying the ancient art of knot making. If he is old the knot maker will sit under the tree with his fellow knot makers—by day, never at night—trading the secrets of knot making and rolling fibers into thread and threads into strands and strands into the ropes that are used to make knots. If the knot maker is young and has not yet mastered his craft he will sit on the periphery of this shade at a slight distance from where the red handed knot makers are sitting. And there he will listen to their talk. Patiently, the young knot maker will listen and watch out of the corners of his eyes as the hands of the old men bend and tuck, noticing without noting their every twist and tug, the sly movements of their fingers that are meant to keep him from picking up the key turns of a knot. Because the Old People do not believe that knowledge should be given to a person who does not already have it or that it should be given freely without seeing a true respect for the effort, the young knot maker will never be taught the ways of knot making but will have to learn instead through careful observation. But because watching a knot being made will only bring a bad end to the knot—causing it to slip or break or to be used against itself—the young knot maker must learn to tie his knot not by watching it being made but by noticing everything else: by observing the things around it. Without daring to look directly the future maker of knots will study the twists and turns that are the pith of his people; and in this way the knot maker will learn his legacy, out of the corners of his eyes, in the same way that the old knot makers once learned theirs. Sitting on the periphery of the tree's shade he will come to know the power of this most ancient art:

that a simple rope looped back through itself can be used to tie down a roof against a strong wind or to make a net that catches fish or to guide a falling tree to the ground. He will learn that a knot can be so simple as to be tied with the weakest fingers of the hand yet faithful enough that it cannot be undone no matter how many ways you pull it. One by one he will come to understand not just the functions of his knots but their many meanings as well: how a knot should be tied one way to encourage the birth of a child but another way to ease the passing of an old woman from this life to the other; that tying top over bottom will bind a man to his descendants; but that tying bottom over top will bind them equally to each other. Like his ancestors before him he will come to see why some knots bring things that are good while others bring nothing but bad; how a knot tied with the quiet end of a rope will surely cause a girl to be born, while the same knot tied with the opposite end of the rope—its dark end—will just as surely cause her to be lost.

At this point the knot maker will have been studying the knots of his ancestors for many years and only now after years of quiet observation will the knot maker tie his first knot. None of the older knot makers will ever show him this knot or speak of it or even suggest that there is such a knot to be tied. But one day he will know that it exists and that the time has come to tie it.

And when all of this has happened—when the knot maker has observed his art and is worthy of it and knows that he has the knowledge to tie up a roof with the same ease as a child's belly—when he is finally ready to tie the many knots of his people the young knot maker does this last thing: carefully he tips over the hard stump on which he has been sitting all these years, the stump that was made by a wood carver many generations ago, and without speaking he rolls it from the periphery of the tree's shade to the cool place at its center, to the very place under the knotmaking tree where the older knot makers are sitting on their own stumps trading the ancient secrets of knot making and watching the storytellers of the island go from one end of the village to the other.

As any knot maker can tell you the kwa plant is not a fast growing plant: after a year its head will poke above the ground; after three years it may reach the knot maker's ankles; and only after a generation has gone by will it be as tall as the person who planted it. In time the healthy kwa will grow to be several times the knot maker's own height with large green leaves and many branches of strong sinewy bark. By now the knot maker himself will be many years older, his hands still strong but his back weak. Every morning he will walk to the place where his kwa is growing, never forgetting to give thanks for its growth or to make sure that the plant is getting the water it will need to take its shape. If there are weeds to be pulled he will bend on crumbling knees to pull them. And if there are thanks that must be given he will make sure that they are given. Later in the day when the sun is at its hottest the aging knot maker will go back to sit under the knotmaking tree with the other knot makers. Sitting with their knots in hand the men will listen as a storyteller stops by with his fires to tell the latest stories of the island: that a child has just been born that morning to an adze maker and his wife; that a woman from the village has died from an improperly tied knot; and that the people of the quarry have at last finished their stone ramp under the old umbilical tree near the river. At this the knot makers will nod quietly because it is not unusual for a child to be born; or for an old woman to pass; or for an umbilical tree to be felled for the sake of a seeing man's idol. But later in the day when the afternoon has started to darken and their fire has been put out for the night the old knot makers will linger a while before returning to their homes. And in the fading light they will talk about what they have just heard.

*It is a very large tree*, one of them might say.
*And very old.*
*Do you think it will rain tonight?*
*The clouds are thick.*

*There are many holes to be dug.*
*And stakes to be driven.*
*But what if the shadow fish goes through the net?*
*It is not easy to tie a good knot.*

From one rainy season to the next the kwa plant outgrows its hole until at last it is tall and strong and has taken its shape. It takes a wisdom beyond the wisdom of the knot maker to know for sure that the kwa has taken its full shape and so when he thinks the kwa plant is ready to be cut down the knot maker continues the making of his knot by calling on the seeing man who will come with his things of prayer to the place where the kwa plant was planted more than forty years ago. Here the seeing man will position himself on the hard ground and with his things in hand pray for the signs that only he can feel: the movement of blood and water that will tell him that this kwa plant is ready to be taken. And if he agrees after many days of prayer that the fibers of this plant are truly ready for the taking the seeing man will look quietly toward the tree cutters who will then cut down the plant. For several long moments there will be a deep silence as the knot maker looks at the bleeding plant and thinks about what has just been done, what has just been taken away: the plant, all its flesh and marrow and sinew, has just been taken away forever and given, forever, to the knot maker with his knot, to the storyteller with his fires, and to the seeing man with the prayer that he is praying. Over the coming days the knot maker will strip the bark of the kwa plant and with aging fingers peel the long strips of the plant from one end to the other. It is from doing this—peeling the strips of kwa from one end to the other—that the knot maker's hands will turn the dark red that is the ancient color of knot making. In younger days the red might have been washed out of his skin by spending much time in the river or in the sea, but now that he is older the red of his hands will be as much a part of his skin as the deep brown of his back.

When the fibers have been stripped and sorted and left for some time to churn in the shallow waters of the sea the knot maker will hang these fibers and brush them and leave them to dry under the cool shade of the village's knotmaking tree. The fibers will now be clean and smooth and as pale as the knot maker's beard. After more than forty years of waiting for the kwa to take its shape the knot maker finally has the fibers that he can use to make the rope for his knot. Because the Old People understand that the journey from fiber to rope can never be untraveled and that a journey of this sort can only be truly worthwhile after the gathering of much time the knot maker will not start to make his rope right away but instead will leave his fibers to hang from the lowest branches of the knotmaking tree. It takes many planting seasons for hanging fibers to become ready for rope and so during the hanging time the knot maker will wait for that day to come by sitting on his wood stump and devoting his time to mastering the ancient art of knot making.

By now the people of the village will know to look for the knot maker under the knotmaking tree and their many requests for knots will have been finding him over the course of much salt traded. But because the Old People have more knots to tie than knot makers to tie them—and because there is far more salt in the sea than fibers under the knotmaking tree—the knot maker, when asked to tie a knot, will not simply tie the knot that has been asked for and be on his way, but will first make sure that the person doing the asking is worthy of the tying. If it is a fishing net to be made the knot maker will be sure to remember each of the fish that this fisherman in need of a net has ever caught. And he will remember when each of these fish were caught and where they were caught and how they were used by the people of the island, whether as sustenance or as tribute. If the knot is for an adze maker the knot maker will look not only at all the adzes that this adze maker has ever made but also at each of the things that has ever been made by the adze maker's adzes: every digging tool and weapon and stake to be driven into the ground; all the sacred idols and stilts and fishing boats for the men who make their living as fishermen. In this way the knot maker will know the real value of every net that has been made and every hole that has been dug and every stone given and every offering of salt and every fire and every tool and every prayer. He will know the legacy of every child that has been born and every tree that has been felled and every roof that has been tied so as to last through the strongest winds of the windy months. Having tied the island's knots for so long the knot maker will know the exact length, if not the exact location in the caves, of the adze maker's hidden knot of ancestry and descent. It is for the knot maker to know all these things so that if he decides after much remembering that the knot being asked for is worthy of the tying only then will he set about the making of the knot.

*Here is a shadow fish*, a young adze maker might say one day as the knot maker is working on a knot for the umbilical tree that will soon be cut down. *It is female and would fit perfectly into the hole that has been dug over by the salt beds where the salt makers make their salt.* Without looking up from his knot the knot maker will nod and over the next few months he will consider the request that has been made. And when the request has been duly considered and the knot maker has seen that the adze maker is worthy of having the knot and that the knot being asked for is worthy of being tied the knot maker will wait under the knotmaking tree for a sign that the time for the knot has come. When that time is at hand he will make his way to the quarry where the adze maker has his house and once there he will stand in silence with the adze maker who gave him the fish. Inside, the midwives will have just brought the carried child from the other world to this one and are now ready for the knot maker to do his work: as the Old People know that no life can pass from one world to another without a knot to separate the two, the midwives will be holding out the half born child and waiting with their basket of birth residue for the knot maker to tie his knot.

In time the blood will be buried and the knot will fall away. The seed will outgrow its hole. The child whose knot is being tied will become strong and firm and will grow into a man who can dig holes or catch fish or carve wood. Or she will grow into a woman who can take brine and soothe muscles and carry children from one world to the next. By now the midwife will be waiting for the knot maker to tie his knot and it is here that he will stand to the side and give thanks. For the salt making. For the knot tying. For the holes that have been dug. For the story that will be told. And when this is done he will begin tying the knot that means the child is ready to become a child. Over the next few moments—while the salt makers are gathering salt to mark this occasion and the storytellers are starting the celebratory fires of the village and the seeing man still sits on the ground with his various things of prayer—the knot maker will begin tying the child's knot of passage, the knot that will mark the upcoming journey from one life to another. And as the knot maker works to make this knot, his hands looping and tucking the knot into shape, the midwives will avert their eyes. The woman on the floor will hold out her arms ready to accept the child that she has been carrying. And the men with the firemaking tools—their firemaking tools still smoldering—will eye the bloody fibers of this birth waiting for the exact moment when the knot maker has finished his knot so that their storytelling can begin.

ᴏ꒰

When the kwa fibers have finally taken their full shape and are ready to become rope the knot maker sits down on his wood stump to begin making the rope that will one day be used to tie his knot. Carefully he lays the long fibers across his lap and holding the ends between the tips of his fingers prepares to roll the thin fibers together. By now it is late afternoon—a good time of day to work with raw kwa fibers—and the sun is trickling through the lowest leaves of the knotmaking tree. A few steps from the tree a fire has burnt down to embers; a storyteller will soon be coming by to put it out for the day.

*Here is some salt that you might care for*, a friend will say as the knot maker is rolling the fibers into threads and the threads into strands. And when the knot maker has set aside his work so that the friends can do their trading—several grains of simple salt for one that is sacred or several that are quiet for a few that are dark—the friend of the knot maker will once again bring up the matter of the knot, asking, in passing, whether the knot maker himself has ever thought that the place down by the old umbilical tree might be a good place for a hole.

*It just so happens*, the knot maker will likely say, *that this may be so*.

The friends will trade salt and the salt will be traded and in this way the very salt that was first given by the knot maker many years ago—the first request for a hole to be dug—will have made its way back to the place under the knotmaking tree where the seeds of all digging are sown.

When his friend has left him the knot maker will return to the fibers that he is rolling. By now his rolled fibers will be as long as his lap and they will be even longer than that by the time the storyteller comes by to give word that the boy who fell from the tree while trimming branches seems to be getting better; but that the girl who was born to the adze maker has taken a turn for the worst; and that the old umbilical tree down by the river, the one that was to be felled tomorrow, will have to be felled on another day: that first there must be a ceremony of passing for the old woman whose knot was improperly tied.

*A very old woman has died of an improperly tied knot,* the storytellers might have told the people of the village that morning while lighting the morning fires of the day. But by evening their story will have acquired the full weight of the old woman's many waters: *Long long ago in the darkness that comes before rope there once was a knot that needed tying....*

Over the next few days the knot makers will work busily to prepare for the old woman's latest passage from one life to the other. Because it is not good to use a rope for one purpose that was made for another and because no passing between lives can be complete until a knot has been tied to separate the two, the knot makers will not use a rope already made but instead will work throughout the day to make a rope out of the raw fibers of the kwa. From the coming to the going of the sun the knot makers will work at the very edge of their craft to make the old woman's rope of passage, rolling its fibers into threads and threads into strands and twisting the strands together until the rope being made has exactly as much length as the passing woman has girth. From the sun's coming to its going the knot makers will work in the cool shade of the knotmaking tree—and from the sun's going to its coming they will work in the cold darkness of night. Although it is not a good thing for a knot maker to make knots in the night—as this would be the darkest kind of knot making—the Old People have long held that the making of rope for an old woman's passing is the only kind that can be done during the night by a person who is a person of the day, such that if a knot maker is ever seen in the night making knots for the day it can be said, without fail, that he is surely making these knots to mark the passing of an old woman from this life to the other.

At the hour that has been set by the seeing man the knot makers will go with their finished rope to the place near the river where the woman's body has been kept. Since learning of the woman's passing from an improperly tied knot the people of the village will have been coming to this place to do their part. The people of the quarry will have brought a flat slab of stone on which the old woman will be placed during the ceremony. The salt makers will have come with gifts of funeral salt. The wood carvers will have carved a piece of wood into the exact size and shape of the old woman's life. The storytellers, for their part, will have brought enough fire to last throughout the day and enough collective memory to last even longer; together they will give words to the girth of this woman's life: to all

the muscles she has soothed and the brine that she
has taken and the knots that she has tied and the
men that she has made. For several long moments
there will be a hot silence as the Old People look
at the passing woman lying on her stone slab and
think about what is about to take place, what is
being taken away: the woman, all her water and
fiber and salt, is being taken away forever and
given, forever, to the flames of the storyteller's
fire, to the soil of the growing kwa, and to the
river with its leaning umbilical tree and shifting
layers of mud. In time the seeing man will come
with his many things for seeing—his pebbles and
his carved idols and his sacred knots—and he
will say a prayer for the woman and her passing.
In words that only he can hear he will pray for the
journey of the woman from this life to the other;
and for the assurance that the journey has not
begun foolhardily; and for the success of the knot
tying ceremony: that none of the men who do
the tying shall find themselves among the flames
of the burning body; or be charred by them; or
be singed from within by the burning feeling
that comes from having caused an old woman
to burn. At this point in his prayer he will take
the wood that is the shape of the old woman's
life and place it on his shoulder in the form of a
wooden idol. He will whip his own flesh using
the knotty fibers of his sacred ropes; he will crush
the smooth pebbles between his teeth, painfully,

as if it were the grinding of salt into human skin. And when all of this is finished he will pause to wait for the signs that must follow: the change in the course of the wind that will cause the smoke from the storyteller's fire to blow in the way of the old woman's journey. And when the wind is blowing in this very direction the seeing man will look up from his prayer to signal that the journey can begin.

At once there will be a sudden stirring from the villagers. The woman's sons and daughters will lift her body from the stone slab and raise it into the air above them and while it is aloft each person of the village will come with a handful of salt to rub into the woman's skin. Nearby the storytellers will be tending their fires and the knot makers will be waiting with their rope. Handful by handful the salt will be rubbed into the passing woman until the skin of this world has been entirely covered in salt. When each person of the village has rubbed hard salt into soft skin the old woman will be taken to a heavy wooden stake driven into the ground—and here the knot makers will begin the woman's final knot tying ceremony by tying the other knot that separates this life from the other. Taking the rope that they have just made, the knot makers will wrap the center of the rope around the woman and her stake, binding soft flesh to hard wood, beginning at her navel and wrapping in opposite directions, upwards and downwards, round and round, until the body is completely wrapped in rope and the woman is committed to her passing: arms, trunk, legs and neck—everything must be bound in the long rope of the knot makers. With generations of knot making to guide them the knot makers will wrap the body until there is no longer a body left to wrap, only rope—until the old woman herself has become rope. By now the smoke will be profound and the fire will be ready. And when the knot makers have finished the wrapping of this old woman with their rope they will gather together to do one final thing: while the plumes of smoke drift off into the sky and while the children of the village wait silently with their salt and while the people of the village stand watching what will be the beginning of the old woman's journey from this life to the other— while all of this is happening—one of the knot makers will take the end of the rope that has been used to wrap the old woman's upper part and bring it back down around to the front of her body where the navel is. And the other end of the rope, which has been used to wrap her lower part, another knot maker will bring up and around the other way until it too has been crossed in front of the woman's body where the navel is. Here they will hold the two ends of the rope crossed in front of the old woman's navel waiting for the island's eldest knot maker to step forward. Nearby the fire will be making a low burning sound and the storytellers will be stoking it so that once this final knot has been tied the old woman can be placed into the flames to mark the beginning of her journey. In a few moments the knot maker will tie this knot and the woman will begin her passage from this life to the other. But for now the village waits—the children with their salt and the storytellers with their fires—each of them watching without looking as the village's eldest knot maker slowly steps forward to tie his knot.

When the ceremony is over and the woman's journey has begun the knot maker will return to the knotmaking tree where his knot making has been left unfinished. Once again he will sit on the wood stump and spread out the emerging rope across his lap: on one side, fibers; on the other, threads. Now he can return to the rope that he has been waiting to make since he first planted the kwa seed so many years ago. Holding the fibers against the skin of his wrinkled thigh the old knot maker rolls his hand over them and along the length of one thigh so that they twist tightly into each other; the fibers travel from the tips of his fingers to the bottom of his palm and when they can go no further he pinches the place where fiber becomes strand and prepares his fingers to do the same once more. It is this very occasion— the moment in knot making where the voices meet and the many fibers of the world are joined to form threads for strands and strands for rope— that more than any other connects the Old People to their past. Here the generations come together between the knot maker's fingers like a pinch of salt to be scattered; or like many smaller rivers flowing into a deeper and larger one.

And so the knot maker does this over the course of many months until his hands are raw and the threads have become strands and the strands have grown long enough to reach from his wrist to his elbow, from his shoulder to his hips, from his ankles to the knuckles of his hand. In time each of the strands will be long enough to pass from one end of the knotmaking tree to the other and then to circle it many times. When the strands are exactly this long the knot maker will work with his fellow knot makers to twist and join them into each other—the hands of the three knot makers working in perfect rhythm—so that the strands can come slowly together, each gaining in girth and consequence what it has just given up in pliancy and volition. For many days the three knot makers will do this until the strands have become a single rope that is as strong and as long as its purpose, a rope that is thin enough to bend yet thick enough not to be bent. To finish the pulling of this very rough rope into a rope that is very smooth the knot maker then wraps the rope around the trunk of the knotmaking tree and with one hand holding the

dark end of the rope and the other hand holding
its quiet end he begins to pull it back and forth
through the smooth groove that has been worn
into the tree by generations of knot makers pulling
their ropes back and forth. Like those that came
before him, the knot maker will pull from the side
of the tree that first sees the sun's coming to the
side that last sees its going; then just as faithfully
he pulls it back through again: silence then sound
then silence then sound then silence then sound
then silence. To the ancient rhythm of rope making,
he will pull from one side to the other until the
rope is as smooth as the very smoothest kwa fibers
that he stripped and peeled so many years ago. At
last there will be no more pulling to do and no
more rope to make. And suddenly there will be
silence without sound. Now for the first time since
setting out to tie his knot many generations ago
the knot maker can look over the rope that he
has just made: the spiraling strands that reach in
perfect rhythm from one end of the rope to the
other; the spiraling threads that go into each of
the strands; the thinly spiraling fibers that go into
each of the threads. From the simple fibers of the
humble kwa plant the knot maker has made a rope
that is stronger than the strongest wind, as reliable
as the rain, as enduring as the darkest depths of the
Old People's deepest and darkest caves.

Now to finish his rope the knot maker must tie
off its end with a knot that can never be untied.

For any rope being made, this is the most essential of all knots because it must last its entire journey— until the day when the rope itself is coiled and wrapped and burnt down to ash. And so on the day when this most undying of knots is to be tied the knot maker will ask the seeing man to come to the knotmaking tree to bless the knot. The seeing man will come and here he will sit with the rope that would be rope but for the final knot that must be tied in it. The seeing man will sit with his things for seeing—his pebbles and his carved idols and his sacred knots—and he will say a secret prayer for the rope whose navel is about to be tied; and for the knot that will do the final tying; and for the tying of the knot itself. And when this is done the seeing man will hold up the rope so that its coils are over his shoulder and here he will offer up the end of the rope that has not yet been tied up—the dark end—and that in a few short moments the knot maker will tie.

*Here is your rope*, the seeing man will say. *It is waiting for you to tie its knot.*

And the knot maker will look at the rope that he has spent many generations making and that will one day be used to tie his knot. And the knot maker will remember the hole that was dug. And the seed that was planted. And the water that was given to the kwa while it was taking its shape. And the storytellers who gave him fire for his rope. And the wood carver who made the tool for the hole digger to dig his hole. And the hole digger who dug his hole. And the tree cutters who brought down the tree that the wood carver used for his tool. And the men from the ocean who gave him fish. And the women who soothed his wounds. And the adze maker. And the people of the quarry. And the medicine man. And the midwives. And the people of the caves.

Remembering all the hands that have contributed to the making of his rope the knot maker will take the end of the rope that is being held out to him by the seeing man. This is the knot that will make his rope a rope. And while the seer looks on, the knot maker will take the unfinished rope and begin to tie his knot.

By now the knot maker will be old and gray and his hands will be the color of the bleeding kwa plant. His back will be bent from bending over his knots for so many years and his eyes will be nearly blind from rolling the fibers of his world into thread and the threads into strands and the strands into the ropes that are used to make knots. After so many years making knots there will be little that can surprise him in the ways of knot making. For generations he has been tying knots to hold down the roofs of houses; and to hold together the stilts for trimming trees; and to separate this life from the other. He has made ropes to go from one side of a river to another and has tied them up so that the people can cross back and forth.

He has made fishing nets that have been used by the men who make their living as fishermen to catch the fish that feed the island. He has made sacred knots for the seeing man. And lashing for the adze maker. He has been called in to untie knots that were tied by other knot makers who are no longer living and that are so well tied that only an old knot maker can untie them. He has done all of these things and more and now finally he is ready to finish off the knot that he began many generations ago when he drove the stake into the ground for the hole digger to find.

Once again the knot maker steadies himself on the wood stump at the center of the knotmaking tree and begins to make his knot. Carefully he positions his hands so they are out of sight of the young knot maker who is still sitting on the periphery of knot making. As an old knot maker the knot maker knows that it is not good for knowledge to be given freely or without seeing a true respect for the effort; or for the tying of a knot to be looked at directly. And so the knot maker turns his body slightly from the young knot maker sitting on the periphery of the tree and trying to pick up the key turns of his knot. And from the other young knot maker sitting at the opposite end of knot making the knot maker simply covers his knot with his hands as if he were a storyteller sheltering his flame from the wind. Before tying the knot the knot maker must make sure that there are no eyes to ruin his knot and that the wind is not blowing in from the ocean. He must see to it that the fibers have not been left out in the sun to become brittle or in a damp place to become damp—that they have indeed been taken from kwa plants that were taken the way a kwa plant should be taken. He must be sure that the salt to be given has been given and the sun has been consulted and that any words spoken about this knot have been spoken indirectly. And that the rope for the knot to be tied, while waiting to be tied, was never coiled against the sun but always and only in the very direction of the sun itself. He must do all these things so that when he finally does tie the knot he will know that the knot that is tied is a knot worth the tying—a knot that pays homage to the many knot makers who came before him, to the ancestors who tied his ancestral knots and left them to be perpetuated in the caves, to the gods who took a world of patternless darkness and made out of this darkness the endless fibers that can be twisted into rope. Before he ties his knot the knot maker makes sure to pray for those who have contributed to his knot: the knot makers and the wood carvers and the hole diggers and the tree cutters and the people of the salt and the adze maker and the seeing men and the wives of the island and the children and the gods and the winds and the rain and the sun and the soil and the stars and the moon and the mud.

Down by the river the Old People are waiting for this prayer to be prayed. Listening for the sounds of the knot maker's fingers as he begins to tie his knot the tree cutters, with their tree cutting tools raised above their heads, eye the hard neck of the umbilical tree. In the quarry the midwife holds out the child being born whose passage from one life to another must be consummated with a knot. Down by the beach the men who make their living as fishermen wait expectantly for the final knot that will tie off their fishing net. Even the young knot maker who for many years has been sitting on the periphery of the knotmaking tree trying to pick up the key turns of this knot will be waiting and watching, as the old knot maker himself once did, out of the corner of his eye. And the hole digger waits for his knot of tribute to be tied. And the old woman lying quiet on her stone slab awaits the tying of the knot that will send her on her journey. And the stake awaits its knot. And the adze awaits its lashing. And the net awaits its tying. Finally the elderly knot maker takes the rope he has just made and looping it over itself he begins to tuck it into the loop.

And the men with the cutting tools watch his fingers without watching. And the midwife holding up the unborn child follows the knot maker's fingers without looking. And the people of the salt listen. And the hole digger waits. And a childless mother with her arms outstretched closes her eyes so that she can see. And the storytellers with their fires. And the seeing man. And the girl who has just been born to the adze maker and who will one day die from an improperly tied knot. All of them wait as the knot maker begins to tighten his knot. Together the people of the island hold their breath and pray: that this knot will be worthy of all the others that have come before it; that it will be used to its end for a purpose that is true; that it will allow them to start fires that are hot and cut trees that are tall and make digging tools that are as hard and as heavy as stone. Together the Old People close their eyes and pray. For the umbilical tree. For the old woman. For the kwa that has been planted. And the salt that will be traded. And while the Old People offer this prayer the kwa plant continues to rustle in the breeze. The shadow fish swim toward the nets that have been cast. And the funeral fire burns down slowly to ash. It is this moment that has been generations in the making. As the sun slopes and the people of the caves come out to do their nighttime work the Old People give thanks that they have lived through another generation of days and that this one has once again given life. Once again the Old People lower their gazes in silent gratitude knowing that the knot they are tying will not break or slip or be used against itself; that it is not being tied foolhardily or before its time; that this knot that they have been tying for so long really has been worth the tying. Here the seeing man steps forward to scatter a final fistful of salt onto the ground where the Old People have been standing for so long waiting with their eyes averted for this simple knot to be tied.

*It is a good knot*, they will say. *And has certainly been worth the making.*

And then they tie the knot.

ଔ   ଔ   ଔ

# THE DIGGING

ca

Which is not to say that it always happens like this. Sometimes the rain does not fall—even during what should be the rainiest days of the rainy month. With no rain to connect the generations the river will not flood and the mud will not turn thick and the hole digger will not be able to dig his hole on the darkest night of the month. When this happens the hole digger will not dig his hole, the hole will remain undug, and the knot maker will not be able to plant the kwa seed for the fibers that will be used to make his rope. Nor will the adze maker be able to bury the bloody offering for the child that has just been born to him. Standing with the blood in his hands the young adze maker will have no choice but to continue to wait in this place for the hole to be dug. In time the blood will dry and will turn to crust and the female shadow fish that has been caught for the purpose will rot and fall apart. The kwa plant that was to be planted to commemorate the birth will dry up and turn to dust. Worst of all, with his hands covered in crusted blood the adze maker will not be able to visit the caves to tie his child's knot of ancestry and descent. In this way the elaborate rope of his ancestry will be left to sit in the darkness of the caves broken and unfinished.

All the while the hole to be dug down by the aged river will stay undug. While the wood carver waits for the adze maker to make his adze and the hole digger waits for the wood carver to carve his digging tool the ground will lie exactly as it would have had the Old People never taken to making knots: dark and dry and undug. With no hole in which to plant a sapling the umbilical sapling will not be planted at all and in time there will be no umbilical tree to grow very hard and very old and to gradually lean out over the river.

*It would be good*, an old friend might say while trading salt, *if a hole could be dug in that place by the river where no umbilical tree has ever been planted.*

This request will go from friend to friend in the form of salt for salt. But when it reaches the only man in the village who could dig such a hole the hole digger will not be able to dig it because there is no rain and the river has not flooded; and as any hole digger worthy of a digging tool will know, a hole must only be dug after the first big flood of the rainy month when the clouds are thick and the mud is thick and the night is dark enough for digging.

With no hole there can be no wood. With no wood there can be no digging tool. With no tool there can be no hole; and with no hole there can be no fibers for the knot maker's knot, no hole for the adze maker's blood, and no umbilical wood for the wood carver's carved digging tool. In this way the Old People will not be able to make their knots or their adzes or the many carved wooden things of the island: their tools and weapons and stakes to be driven into the ground. The knot maker will be left to sit under the knotmaking tree observing knots already made; the wood carver will have no better thing to do than to wait forty generations for his carved digging tool to age under the icy waters of the river; and the adze maker standing alone near the salt beds, his hands covered in blood, will have no choice but to stand with his bloody offering in hand waiting for his child's hole to finally be dug.

And then it might also happen that after waiting forty generations for the icy river to flow the wood carver will lose sight of the place where he once left his digging tool to harden in the waters of the river. The water will flow over this digging tool for forty generations and the wood will turn as hard and as heavy as stone. Yet when the forty generations have passed and it is time for the wood carver to claim his work he may come to see that the generations have not been kind to his memory, that the river's flow has since changed, the mud has been turned and upturned many times, and that forty generations—even on an island as small as this one—can be a very long time to wait for a digging tool that has been buried.

*Forty generations ago*, he might say to a friend who has come by to trade salt, *a wooden digging tool was buried in the icy river to become as hard and as heavy as stone. It is a very good tool and will dig many good holes.* And here the wood carver will add, in passing, that forty generations is a long time indeed, that mud and water do not necessarily stay where you put them, and that it would be a very good thing if the exact location of this particular digging tool could somehow be remembered.

In better times the wood carver might call upon the island's storytellers to help him recall the exact location of the tool that was buried so many generations ago. But with no dug holes the storytellers will not have any rope to make their fires. With no rope to spin one piece of wood into another there can be no fire. With no fire there can be no silence. And without silence there can be no story.

And so the wood carver will wander along the very long river from one end to the other looking for that certain place in the mud where his carved digging tool was buried. From one place to another he will travel and as he makes his way along the aging river he will be blind to the many requests that have collected back under the tree where he once sat during the day carving wood. Searching for his tool he will not be able to attend to his craft, to make the island's strongest and straightest digging tools and weapons and stakes to be driven into the ground. He will not carve the wooden stump for the young knot maker to sit on while studying the art of knot making. Or the stilts to be used by the tree cutters while cutting trees. Or the boards for trading salt. Or the seeing man's idols. Or the sticks that are used to make fire. Nor will he be able to make the piece of funeral wood that is the exact size and shape of an old woman's life. In time there will be none of these things. And the holes will stay undug; and the digging tools will go unmade; and the stakes marking the place for the knot maker's hole will go uncarved such that when it is time for the knot maker to make his request for a hole there will not be a carved stake to mark its location. Without this stake the hole digger will walk past the unmarked hole without knowing to dig it and in this way the hole will remain undug, the fibers will go unplanted, and the knot, as before, will be left untied.

*It is a shame that no hole has yet been dug,* the Old People might say, *because the place down by the river is very good and would make for a fine umbilical tree someday.*

And then there are times when a knot to be tied might have more than one way of being tied—such that a knot maker sitting under the knotmaking tree prefers his own way of tying while his fellow knot maker sitting across from him prefers another way entirely. If the knot makers are of different ages then the younger knot maker will tie the knot in the way of the older knot maker. But if the knot makers are of the same age and their contributions to knot making are similar each of them may decide that his side of the tree gives the better view of knot making and that for this reason he alone knows the better way to tie a knot. When this happens the knot makers will grow doubtful and will not tie any knot until the kink in their knot making has been unraveled. Because it is not good to tie a knot that may not be true to its tying and because a knot that is in doubt can never be truly tied there will in fact be no way to know which of the two ways of knot tying is the greater. Or which is the lesser. Without tying this knot the knot makers will remain under the knotmaking tree with no knots to tie, such that in time the doubtful knot makers will cease to be knot makers at all. The requests for knots will gather and still the knot makers will sit under the tree with nothing to do but remember knots once made and listen with empty hands as the island's storytellers stop by with their many stories of the island: that the young tree cutter who fell from a tree many years ago is now healthy and strong and wiser in the ways of tree cutting; but that the dry place down by the river is only getting drier and so the hole for the umbilical tree cannot yet be dug. Here the knot makers will learn that the old woman who died from an improperly tied knot has been placed on her stone slab and is lying ready for her final ceremony to begin; but that the child born to the adze maker and his wife may not be born to them at all—that the rope of her navel has yet to be cut and her knot is still waiting to be tied.

*Here is a shadow fish*, a young adze maker might mention one day as the knot maker is sitting idly under the knotmaking tree. *It is female and would fit perfectly into the hole that will surely be dug over by the salt beds just as soon as the rains have returned.*

But when the time for this knot is at hand the knot maker will not go to the quarry where the adze maker has his house. Inside, the midwives will have just brought the half born child from the other world to this one and are now ready for the knot maker to do his work: to tie the most basic of knots—the child's knot of passage to mark the journey from one life to another. As the Old People know that no life can pass from one world to another without a knot to separate the two, the midwives will be holding out the breathless child and waiting with their basket of birth residue for the knot maker to tie this knot. Next to them the childless mother will be lying on her back and holding out her arms, ready to take the child that she has just carried into this world.

*Here is a child worth the carrying*, she will say. *It would be good if a knot could now be tied.*

But it will not be for the knot maker to tie this knot. Instead he will continue to sit under the knotmaking tree with his unfinished rope and his dangling kwa fibers and his belief in a better way of knot tying. And while he sits with these things there will not be a single knot that can be tied on the island. No nets will be made. No rope will be finished. No adze stones will be tied to their handles. In time the only knots to be found on the island will be those that have already been tied many generations ago, in the earliest days of hole digging when the island's original knot maker emerged from warm mud to tie the first knots of the world.

And so while the knot maker sits with his unmade knots under the knotmaking tree the woman on the floor will be left to hold out her arms expectantly for a child that will never come; lost on its journey the unborn child will remain between the other world and this one, eyes closed and navel still attached, waiting for the knot of a knot maker who cannot make knots.

And then sometimes it will happen that a knot maker has chosen the wrong way to tie a knot and that his knot has therefore been tied improperly. If it is a knot to hold an adze stone to its handle it might be that the knot maker tied the knot so the stone slips when it is struck against wood; when this happens the knot will slip, the adze will fail, and the wood to be carved will be left uncarved or disfigured or even broken by the faulty adze. If it is a knot to hold down the roof of a house it might be that the knot was tied in such a way that the roof begins to rattle during a strong wind and in time the knot will give way and the roof will falter. Or if it is a knot to separate one life from another it could be that the knot maker was not careful while doing his tying and tied an unborn girl's knot with the dark end of the rope instead of its quiet end thereby causing her to be lost to her journey before it can even begin.

Understanding that a single faulty knot is sure to spread the seed of many others, the Old People will now know to expect the coming of a new era of improperly tied knots. Soon the shadow fish will begin to pass through the nets of the men who make their living as fishermen. From one side of the net to the other even the largest fish will pass such that when the fishermen take up their nets they will see that their knots have slipped or have broken and that even their most faithful nets have become so thin and so frail that the shadow fish are passing through them easily, like water itself. In silence the fishermen will collect their empty nets and return without fish to the beach where they keep their fishing boats.

When this happens the men who make their living as fishermen will not give in or lose courage but will simply go again with their nets to the place in the ocean where the fish have always come. As fishermen they will know that there have always been fish to be taken into the nets and that there will always be fish to be so taken. And they will know that though the fish may now be keeping to themselves it is only a matter of time before they will once again return and that the shadow fish now passing through their faulty nets will sooner or later be caught. As they have done since their very first days of taking fish from the ocean the fishermen will cast their nets and wait for the fish to come. But once again the fish will not come. And once again the men who make their living as fishermen will collect their empty nets and return without fish to the beach where they keep their fishing boats.

Without fish from the fishing nets the islanders will have no fish to eat and will soon grow weak in flesh and thought. The people of the quarry will not have the strength to carry their stones to the place by the river where the umbilical tree has yet to be planted; the tree cutters will not have the will to climb the trees that need to be cut; and the people of the salt will not have the endurance to withstand the hot days of rainless work that are necessary to make their salt. With no salt there can be no salted fish and without salted fish there can be no tribute to offer the hole digger in exchange for his dug holes. With no holes for their knots the people of the island will grow even hungrier and it is here that they will begin to stray from their ancient ways. Of distinguishing day from night and light from darkness. Of unhurried observation and indirectness. Of never speaking of the unseen using words that are spoken.

*I really need a digging tool,* the hole digger might say to a wood carver during the part of the day when the sun can be neither up nor down. *Could you please make one for me?*


At this the Old People will be changed. The clouds that may have been gathering on the horizon will thin out and pass over the island without leaving their rain. The sun will scorch any seed that has been planted. The fragile kwa plant whose seed was placed into its hole many years ago by the young knot maker will choke and wither and return to the dry soil as dust. Even the river of the island—as ageless as it is—will become narrow and sluggish from one season to the next. In time the women of the island will notice that the generations have ceased to flow through them and that their bodies have become as dry and as barren as the hands of the tired adze maker still standing alone with the blood of his child's birth.

And the young girls will not be born. And young boys will not be brought forth. And in time there will be no children and no plants and no trees. There will be no knots and no fires and no nets. There will be no mud and no holes. There will be no salt and no smoke. There will be no prayer. Across the island there will be nothing but cold silence during the night and dead heat during the day.

Here the island's storytellers will pass through the village bearing witness to the knot that was improperly tied. Without the tools to make their fires the storytellers will have no story of their own to tell; instead they will see the knot maker sitting in silence under the village's knotmaking tree with no fibers for his ropes, no ropes for his knots, and no true way of tying a knot that needs tying. They will see the wood carver wandering along the dusty river bed looking for the digging tool that was buried forty generations ago. Down by the salt beds they will see the poor old adze maker, his hair gray and his bloody hands now wrinkled, still mourning the child that would not be born to him many years ago. Walking further into silence the storytellers will see the fishermen unloading their empty nets. And the people of the quarry sitting tired and hungry on the heavy stones of their quarry. They will see shriveled old women and waterless young girls. They will see stooped men standing with their disaffected sons. And if they should walk down to where the water used to flow they will see the shallow bed of the dying river where the rain no longer goes; and the dried mud near its banks where nothing overflows; and the bare field down by the river's path where it seems no plant can grow. They will see a world of severed knots and crumpled roofs and failed and discarded nets. They will see fibers not stripped. And stones not moved. They will see the dried bones of the old woman who was placed on her stone slab many years ago but who could not be sent on her journey without the wood of the wood carver, the fire of the storyteller, and the final knot across her navel that was left untied by the island's eldest knot maker. In time the storytellers will see all these things, and they will notice.

And they will remember.

ﻭ

And then it might occur that just when it seems to the Old People that things cannot get any worse— when it seems that nets can get no emptier nor the river any drier—things can in fact get much worse. That the rains will continue to not come— not just through the rainy months of this year but through the rainy months of many years. And that the wood carver in his search for his digging tool will have gone from one end of the river to the other—from the top of the mountain to the edge of the sea—without finding the digging tool that was buried. And that each of the knot makers is still holding to his own way of knot tying such that in time the knots will cease to be tied at all. And the waters will cease to flow. And the holes of the island can no longer be dug.

In time there will be nothing for the storytellers to see but midwives trying in vain to catch fish and people of the quarry trying vainly to carve wood. They will see hole diggers trying to cut trees and fishermen struggling to make fires and tree cutters using their cutting tools to bring unborn children from one life to another. They will see old women tying knots and children telling stories. They will see salt that is simple traded for salt that is sacred. And salt that is sacred traded for nothing in return. From deep within the caves they will hear the sounds of knots being tied to the wrong knots, by the wrong hands, in the wrong way—so that, in time, these knots will tell a story of ancestry and descent that is new and bold and different.

When these things happen the Old People will know that there are things befalling them that are not theirs. And that if these new things are left to age they will cease to be new at all but will instead become proper descendants of the older things. At this the Old People will ask the seeing man to come to the place by the river bed where the river used to flow. Because it is not good to make a request of a seeing man directly—or even to speak indirectly of things that cannot be seen—the Old People will never truly ask for the seeing man's wisdom but instead will expect him to hear the many words not spoken. And when he has heard this request not made and is ready to answer this call not issued he will come to the place by the river where no rain has come and no water is flowing.

In the driest days of the hottest month the seeing man will sit on the dusty ground and pray to feel the things that only he can feel: the hidden waters that move deep below the dry mud of the river and the generations that have flowed for so long through the people of the island. Here the man will sit with his things for seeing—his pebbles and his carved idols and his sacred knots— and he will hold them between his fingers in the way that seeing men do. And in the deepest of all prayers he will pray to understand what it is about the ways of the island that has caused these new things to take place: why the rains have stopped falling; why the digging tool cannot be found; and why two knot makers sitting under the same knotmaking tree cannot agree on a simple knot that needs tying. By now all sounds of the island will have fallen away so that while the seeing man sits on the hot ground of prayer the Old People can wait in quiet silence for the ancient voices to be heard. The fishermen will have stopped their fishing. The storytellers will have stopped their wandering. Even the children of the island will be sitting without stirring and waiting with their parents for the unseen voices to come.

In deep prayer the island's seer will continue to sit with his things for seeing and pray through the hottest time of the day when the sky is tall and the sun is at its peak; and he will do this through the coldest and darkest time of the night when the sun is down and the empty skies send the world's cold into his bones. Without noticing the coming or the going of the light around him the seeing man will stay deep and heavy in his prayer with his eyes closed and his thoughts upturned and his hands resting gently on the things that help him see: the idol that was carved many years ago by the wood carver; the pebbles given gratefully by the people of the quarry; and the sacred knots— the many faithful knots tied in the ancient ways by the island's eldest knot makers. And if after many days of prayer his prayer has been a worthy one the vision he needs will come to him like sudden rain; and here it will become clear why it is that so many new things have happened on the island: why it is that the rains no longer fall and the women no longer bear children. Why the holes cannot be dug and the fires cannot be made. Why salt is no longer traded and stones no longer given. Why the adze flies off its handle and the shadow fish go through the nets. Why the carved tool falters during use but the weapon remains straight and true. And why after dying from an improperly tied knot the old woman has been left to rot on the stone slab of her journey.

*These new things are happening*, the seeing man will explain, *because other things have happened*.

And here with his eyes still closed the seeing man will name the other things that have happened to bring these new things upon them. That a kwa plant has been cut without the blessing of the seeing man. Or a digging tool has been given to a hole digger who is not worthy of his art. Or the tree cutters, standing ready to cut down the old umbilical tree leaning out over the river, did not wait for the knot maker to complete his knot and began their cutting before its time— before the knot was fully tied. Or it could be that a young knot maker sitting on the periphery of the knotmaking tree once leaned forward on his wood stump and while trying to pick up the key turns of a knot looked directly at the knot as it was being tied. Or the cause of the new things might be something as distant as the improper tying of an old woman's knot: that many years earlier a midwife holding out the adze maker's child to a knot maker that would not come grew impatient; and that with no knot maker to tie off the girl's knot of passage she took it upon herself to tie with her own hands this most basic of knots— the knot that separates this life from the other. It might be that a request for a digging tool was not made indirectly. Or that it was improperly carried out. Or that a hole was dug during the day. Or wood carved at night. Or trees incorrectly taken. Or fiber gathered before its time. Or it could be that the ancestors were not honored. Or thanks not given. Or prayers not prayed. It might be that words and fire were allowed to mix. Or knowledge given to someone who did not already have it. In fact it could be any of these things that has caused so many new things to take place. Or it could be all of them at once.

*It is a very long river,* the midwives might say while holding out the unborn child to a knot maker who will never come.

*And very old.*
*Do you think it will rain tonight?*
*There are no clouds.*
*But there are so many fires to be made.*
*And stories to be told.*
*But what if the blood of this birth turns to dust?*
*It is not easy to dig a good hole.*


With his eyes still closed the seeing man will continue his prayer by praying over the things that have been taking place on the island: for the tool that has been lost; for the knot that cannot be tied; for the rain that will not come. Here he will take the digging tool and place it on his shoulder in the form of a wooden idol; he will whip his own flesh using the knotty fibers of his sacred ropes; he will crush the smooth pebbles between his teeth, painfully, as if it were the grinding of hard stake into hard earth. And when all of this is finished he will pause to wait for the signs that must follow: the distant smell of rain that will tell him where the water dwells and why it has been so slow to come to the island as rain. Here he will understand that the buried digging tool is not lost after all—that it is exactly where it was put forty generations ago and that it is ready to be claimed by the wood carver. With his eyes closed to the world the seeing man will come to see that there is no knot—no matter how cleverly or improperly tied—that cannot be untied and retied so as to be tied in a better way. And that it is the tying itself that makes the knot worth its making.

At last the seeing man will set down his things for seeing and here he will open his eyes to a blinding sun. Against the ancient light he will open his eyes and as the wisdom of the generations courses through him like blood through umbilical cord he will come to see what must be done to make the waters flow once again. *The waters will flow anew*, the voices will say, *And the plants will once again grow. Women will give birth and dying embers will glow to become fire and fish will go where they always go. All of this is sure to happen just as it has always happened before. Just as the waters have always flowed and the rivers have always flooded. But before any of these things can happen—before the holes of the island can be dug, before the fires of the world can be made—there is a thing that must first be done.*

Here the Old People will be listening for the quiet words of the seeing man:

*To make the waters flow*, the seeing man will say, *there is a knot that must be tied.*


At this the Old People will be lost. For surely no knot can be tied if there is no true way to tie it. Sitting in the shade of the knotmaking tree the knot makers will be looking at each other across the fateful knot resting on the ground between them. After many years of sitting idly and not tying their knots the knot makers can only remember the bygone days when their knots could be tied wholeheartedly. The days when their fibers were long and strong. And their knots were strong and true.

*It is a shame we have this thing between us*, the knot makers will sigh, *because it would be good if we could tie our knots again.*

Hearing this request the seeing man will go to the place by the knotmaking tree where the fibers have been hung to age in the breeze and there he will call the idle knot makers together. To unravel the kink in their knot making he will suggest that they bring to the knotmaking tree every knot that they have ever tied: every adze and every net; every knot for a stake; and every rope that has been made from the fibers of the humble kwa plant.

Over the coming months the knot makers will bring the knots from their nets and their adzes and every other knot that can be taken into the hand and they will hang them from the knotmaking tree one by one until the tree itself is covered in knots. The tree will be draped in knots and when this has been done the seeing man will encourage the knot makers to bring to the tree every knot of passage they have ever tied—every rope to mark the passing from one life to another. Dutifully each knot maker will bring every child whose knot he has tied—every child of the village and every older person of the village who has since grown from a child being born into a tree cutter or adze maker or salt maker, or who has grown from breathless beginnings to soothe wounds and listen to stories and take into herself the brine of her fathers—such that in time the many knots collected can be seen out of both corners of the eye: one for each of the knot makers. In this way each knot maker will have given flesh to the knots that he has tied and the passages he has made possible; and in this way he will lay out, for the seeing man to see, his exact contribution to the art of knot making. Now when there are no more knots to be laid out the knot makers may find that there are still many knots that have been made but that cannot be taken into the hand or carried to the tree to embody a contribution to knot making: every bridge or roof or knot of

an old woman who has long since passed. Every
knot that has been given as tribute. Every rope
that has been coiled against the sun and then
burnt down to ash. And so, to remember these
knots, a knot maker will rely upon the storyteller
to tell the many stories of the knots that have been
tied and the genealogies that have been preserved:

*Many years ago*, the storyteller might recall, *there
was a knot that needed tying....*


In time the knotmaking tree will be completely
covered in knots: the knots will hang from the tree
like heavy fruit and in time its branches will bend
low from the weight of so much knot making.
When the day of unraveling is upon them the
people of the island will come to the tree to learn
which of the knot makers has made the better
knot. Here they will stand behind the knot maker
who has tied their own knot of passage such that
the two gatherings will stretch from the center of
the knotmaking tree all the way to the flat of the
horizon. Because the Old People understand that
life does not begin with birth and because they
know that birth is not the beginning of life the
Old People will not stand by themselves when
they stand but will stand at the head of the many
ancestors who came before them, the unbroken
chain of knots stretching back to the deepest
darkest places in the caves. In this way the seeing

man will see much further than these progeny now branching out from the knotmaking tree toward the horizon, but all the way back to the generations that have come before—the many knots of ancestry and descent that make up each of these people whose knots the knot maker has tied.

At last the seeing man will be ready to trace the broken knot back to its narrowest fibers, to reveal which of the knot makers is the better maker of knots. Looking over the knots that have been hung from the tree the seeing man will remember when each knot was tied, who tied it, and for what purpose. One by one he will remember how a net was used, the fish it caught, the people it fed, and the things that were made by the people then fed by these fish: the adzes made and holes dug; the salt traded and wood carved. He will remember each of the knots that have been given to the nighttime hole digger and the many holes dug and the many trees planted and the many tools made and the many stories told. He will remember whether these planted umbilical trees were used to make tools that were themselves used to make holes that were good; or whether they made holes that were used against themselves. Here the seeing man will remember each of the children whose knots were tied and all the deeds that they have done. And he will remember all that was done by their fathers; and by their mothers; by the many ancestors that have come before them—and by the many descendants who will come after. Looking past the tree back into the caves of his people he will remember not just the many knots of passage that were tied by the knot makers but also the contributions that these many knots have made to the knot maker's knot in return: the hole digging and adze making and tree cutting. The brine taking and child bearing and wound soothing. The storytelling and firemaking. The kwa planting and stone gathering. Over time he will remember all of this and in this way the seeing man will know the true value of every knot that has ever been tied on the island and the value of every hole that has been dug and every stone given and each grain of salt traded and every silence honored and every tool and every idol and every stilt and every prayer. He will know the legacy of every child that has been born and every tree that has been felled and every roof that has been tied so as to last through the strongest winds of the windy months. Having unraveled the island's entanglements for so long the seeing man will know the exact length of the knot maker's hidden knot of ancestry and descent and whether it has been a rope worth the making; and in this way he will know the full contribution—the true legacy—of the knot maker himself. It is for the seeing man alone to know these things. And so when all of this has been done the seer will run his fingers over the knots of the opposing knot makers—over the threads that make up the strands and the strands that make up the rope—and here he will pronounce the words that will allow the knot makers to once again tie their knots.

*Each of you is a knot maker who has tied many good knots*, the seeing man will say, *but it is clear that the greater knot is this one....*

At last the seeing man will hold up the better knot. And with that the kink in the island's knot making will be unraveled.


And all the while the trees of the island choke and wither from the heat. The sun rises and falls but then rises yet again. The ocean crawls up to the place near the salt beds where the salt makers will one day make their salt. And then it crawls back out. It has been the hottest part of the day for some time and the land is smoldering. The air is still. In the blinding heat that comes before fire making, the thin clouds move across the sky. But the winds of the island do not blow back and forth. The sun blazes over the place near the beach where the salt makers have decided to make their salt. The earth gathers the heat. The plants wilt against the sun. The umbilical sapling to be planted down by the river cannot grow or spread and instead turns to dust. The rains that used to fall in the mountains no longer make their way to the sea, to the place where the salt makers have decided to dry their salt. The rain ceases to flow from the top of the mountain to the bottom of the sea, the generations no longer pass to connect them, and the river that used to flow so endlessly becomes as dry and as pitiless as salt. The shadow fish pass through the nets. The storytellers find no flame for their fire. In time the generations rot on the stone slabs of the island like the bones of a forgotten old woman whose knot has been improperly tied. A sand crab is picking at the flesh. The knots of ancestry and descent lie broken and unfinished in the quiet darkness of the caves. Amid the long silence that comes before storytelling the elderly knot maker is stepping forward to tie his knot.

ᏣᏅ

And so this is how the Old People begin to dig their hole: first they make a fire. Because no fire should be given to a person who does not have a true connection to silence—as this would make for the worst kind of digging—the Old People will never ask that a fire for a hole be made outright. And because it is not a good thing for a person who is not a storyteller to handle fire—just as it is equally unspeakable for a person who has not handled fire to tell stories—a person who needs a fire but is not a storyteller will not dare to make this fire himself but will instead go to a friend to trade salt. Here the person in need of fire will mention, in passing, that he has brought some salt of his own to trade and hearing of the need for salt his friend will take out the salt trading board that was given by the wood carver long ago in return for this or that stone of the island. Because no two pieces of salt can ever be the same the two friends will lay out their salt by size and texture and kinship: simple salt to one side, sacred salt to the other. In this way salt of similar shape will be admired for its similarity and salt of uneven ancestry will be sorted and studied and traded such that by the time the two men are done giving salt for salt each will have received an amount that has made his own salt more suited to the trading that must now be done: to request a knot for an adze; to honor a rope that has been made; or, in the case of the wood carver, to find his lost digging tool.

*It is a very good collection of salt*, a wood carver might say about the salt that has just been traded. *And it should certainly help find the digging tool that was buried in the cold mud of the river so many generations ago.*

Here the wood carver will thank his friend for the salt and with his own salt in hand go back to the tree where he once spent his days carving the wood things of his island—tools and weapons and idols and stilts and wood that is the size and shape of an old woman's life. Knowing that salt is not a thing to be traded hastily or before its time the wood carver will have many months to wait for his salt to reach the storytellers. And so while he waits he will continue to search the length of the very long river for his lost digging tool.

*Forty generations ago*, a friend might be saying over salt being traded, *a wooden digging tool was buried in the icy river to become as hard and as heavy as stone. But forty generations is a very long time. Mud and water do not tend to stay where you put them. And so it would be a very good thing if the exact location of this lost digging tool could somehow be remembered.*

In time the wood carver's request for fire will travel from one friend to another until it finally reaches a storyteller who will then weigh the request. And when after much remembering this storyteller has decided that the wood carver is worthy of the request being made, the storyteller will gather his firemaking tools—the curved bow and the two pieces of wood and the thin rope to spin them into each other—and he will make his way to the place by the lifeless river where the wood carver has been searching. There he will bend down on the dry dust and begin to make his fire. Carefully he will set the pointed end of one wood stick into the flat side of the other and with the rope that has just been given to him by the knot maker he will pull the rope back and forth, faster and faster, spinning wood into wood until the wood itself becomes hot. The wood carver, meanwhile, will be listening for the sound of wood on wood. And while the storyteller is using his rope to spin the sticks into fire the wood carver will be told of the latest happenings of the island: that the wife of the adze maker has not stopped holding out her arms for the child that she lost so many years ago; but that an elderly knot maker has finally stepped forward to tie the old woman's knot of passage.

At last the heat from the spinning will glow: and for the first time in many years there will be a fire burning outright on the island. At this the wood carver will grow silent, thankful for the fire and for its light and for its warmth. Because fire and words should never mix too closely and because a wood carver will always have more need for fire than for words—though more fear of words than fire—the wood carver will keep a wary silence near this hot flame that is now burning outright.

In time the fire will burn down to ash and it is here that the storyteller will once again resume his storytelling by telling the story that will allow the wood carver to find his tool and the hole digger to dig his hole. From one grain of salt to the next the storyteller will tell the long story of the digging tool that was buried in the icy water forty generations ago: about the darkness that comes before hole digging and how before there could be any holes there first had to be fire. And how, to make their fires, the Old People first had

to make a rope that could be used to make fire—
and how the first knot ever tied was tied to make
such a rope. Over time the storyteller will tell the
story of the island's first knot maker and of every
knot that the knot maker's knots have ever made:
every fire that was started; every roof that was tied
down; every child whose passage from one life to
the next was commemorated with a knot. From
silence to mud to rope to knot to wood to words
to fire the storyteller will tell the story of the island
and of how, one day forty generations ago, an old
wood carver took a carved wooden tool to a place
down by the river and buried it deep in the mud.
And here the storyteller will tell the story that has
been passed from one generation to the next: the
story of the long rope that lies hidden in the caves
and that with each child born becomes one knot
longer.

That night the people of the caves will come
out to do their unseen work. From his sleep the
wood carver will be led to the place near the
river where the carved digging tool is buried and
here he will be shown the exact place in the mud
where the digging tool was left to harden. Because
it has never happened that a day person has seen
a person of the night the wood carver—who is a
day person—will not actually see the people of
the caves but will go to the river with his eyes
closed; and there, with his eyes closed, he will
see the digging tool that has been left for him.

The next day the wood carver will return to the same place in the river where forty generations ago his fellow wood carver sunk the piece of wood into the cold mud of the river—the place that was shown to him during the night by the people of the caves—and here he will find the tool which is now as hard and as heavy as stone. His tool in hand the wood carver will say a silent prayer for the wood that has finally been found, for the story just told, and for the people of the caves who, once again, have done their nighttime work.

At last the wood carver has the tool that he has been seeking for so long and that can at last be given to the hole digger to dig his hole. Now the wood carver can take the carved digging tool that he himself carved many years ago and that he has been carrying with him during his search and with a silent prayer place it into the same mud to become as hard and as heavy as the tool that he has just found. That night the tired wood carver will sleep knowing that his work is finally done. That it has been done well. And that in forty generations it can be unearthed by a fellow wood carver and given in the same way and with the same dusty search to a nighttime digger of holes. In the morning the wood carver will go to the tree to see that the coil of knots and digging tool have been claimed during the night and to pick up the small offering of salt and the bundle of dried fish that the hole digger has left him as tribute to his work.

*It is a very good tool that the wood carver has made,* the Old People will say, *and has definitely been worth the searching.*

૱

Then one day it happens: while walking through the dusty field by the river the storyteller looks up to see the gray clouds forming above the island. By now the smell of coming rain will be making its way over the island and the Old People will begin to sense that this time, after so many years of sun and heat, the rain truly is going to come. The air will have grown thick and heavy and the winds have begun to swell. The trees begin to rustle in the wind and a cool and forgotten air blows across the island—from the side of the world where the sun has always risen to the side where it will always set.

Across the island the Old People will not move lest the rains become weary and change course. Standing where they have been standing, the Old People will wait in silence for the rain to come. The fishermen on the beach will stand with their fishing nets, unwilling to move. The people of the quarry will be waiting in their quarry as motionless as the stones around them. The midwife will stay very still as she holds out the child that has just been born. And the adze maker standing alone in the field will continue to stand with his bloody hands and his dried kwa plant looking up toward the clouds that are now becoming thicker and heavier on the horizon.

Down by the dusty river the seeing man will be sitting with his ancient things of worship—his pebbles and his carved idols and his sacred knots—and he will be saying a prayer for the rain that is approaching. That it will not fail to fall on the many dry places of the island. Or to water the withered kwa plant. Or to gather in the mountains and to eventually make its way to the sea. That the generations will once again begin to flow through the women of the island and that the river will once again flood so that the dusty field down by the archaic river can turn, as it always has, to mud.

Here the clouds will grow even thicker and the air will grow heavier. The wind will move even louder through the trees, shaking the many knots that still hang from the village's original knotmaking tree. Like leaves of an earlier time, the knots will shake and rattle in the wind leaving the old knot makers to wait under their knotmaking tree for a rain that has not come at all since it last came many generations ago.

And the leaves of the umbilical sapling will rustle in the growing winds. And the leaves of the drying kwa plant will begin to shake. The fibers that hang from the knotmaking tree will be stirring in the wind while the knot makers sit motionless and wait. The storytellers will have gathered up their firemaking tools and are now standing with their tools waiting for the rain. And the women of the island will wait in their houses, their waters beginning to stir but their wombs still dry. And the tree cutters will be waiting atop their stilts. And the people of the quarry will wait. And the adze maker. And the seeing man who has been sitting for so long on the reverberating ground of prayer.

That night the rain will begin to fall. At first it will come in small drops that pelt the dusty ground and leave dark round holes in the dry dirt. Then gradually it will increase through the night until by morning it is coming down so hard that the fishermen cannot see past the gray rain to the ocean beyond their fishing boats. The mountains at the top of the island will be hidden by clouds and rain. Even the sun will be blackened so that the island has become the darker color of stone and water. For many days the rain will fall until the ground around the river bed has turned to slick mud and the river itself begins to stir. From the top of the mountain to the bottom of the sea the river will gradually flow—first through shallow channels and then in a single shallow stream and then after many more days of rain as a rush of water coming down from the mountains to the sea. While the rain continues to fall the river will rise until it spreads out over the banks that only a few days ago were dead and lifeless. And here the ground around the river will puddle and stream as the river begins to flood its banks.

At this the Old People will know that the rain has not wearied and will not change course, that it has indeed come to stay. And still they will stand where they are standing and wait for the rain to take hold. Huddling under the knotmaking tree the knot makers will wait for the rain to finish its course. The salt makers will stand in their flooded salt beds. And the women of the island will wait patiently in their homes as the waters begin to flow around them and within them. Standing alone near the briny salt beds the adze maker will feel the dried blood being washed from his skin onto the wet ground; in his hands the withered kwa plant is regaining life.

At last the seeing man will open his eyes and gather up the things that have helped him see: the pebbles and the carved idols and his many sacred knots. And with this the people of the island will be overjoyed. Gradually they will begin to stir from their stances—to shake out the quiet from their legs. And the village will come alive: the fishermen running through the rain with their nets; the midwives screaming in joy at the waters now flowing; and the children of the island after standing still for so long finally rushing outside to make their play in the sliding rain.

That night the hole digger will go down to the field where the seeing man has been sitting and there he will see a stake driven into the ground. And he will notice it. And he will know that a hole should be dug in that place and that on the darkest night of the month he should go with his digging tool—the one that was just found and given to him by the wood carver—to dig the hole that was requested many years ago: the hole that the knot maker needs to tie his knot. And while he waits for the darkest night of the month the hole digger will take his digging tool and make his way to the place by the salt beds where another hole must be dug—the hole for the adze maker to bury the blood that he has been holding for so long.

And he will dig it.


At this the island will be reborn. While the rains fall and the river flows the people of the island will begin the long journey back to the ways of their ancestors: of distinguishing day from night and light from darkness. Of purposeful observation and indirectness. Of hearing words not spoken. Of revering the things that stay, above the things that come and go. The adze maker at last will have the hole that he needs. And here he will bury the blood that he has been holding all these years. Carefully he will put it into the hole along with the salt, the shadow fish, and the tiny seed of the kwa plant to mark the birth. Now he can go to the place where his family's ancestral rope is hidden in the cool and quiet darkness of the caves and here, in darkness, he will trace along its length until he finds his own knot and onto this knot—the knot tied by his father—he will tie the knot of his son.

At home his wife will be overjoyed to see her husband after all these years and here she will take his adze and soothe his muscles and listen to his long story of standing. That night she will open her womb to the rivulets of brine that pour out. And she will turn these waters into the young girl whose knot is waiting to be tied by the elderly knot maker and whose blood has just been buried over by the salt beds in the hole just dug.

In the morning the adze maker will make the adze that was requested so many years ago. And he will give this adze to the wood carver who will then use it to carve a digging tool for the hole digger. From adze maker to wood carver to hole digger the waters will continue to flow until it happens during the darkest night of the month that the hole digger once again comes across the stake that has been driven into the ground in that place by the river where the first big flood has turned the mud thick. And on this night when the clouds are thick and the mud is thick and the night is dark enough for digging the hole digger will dig the hole for the umbilical sapling to be planted.

And the umbilical sapling will be planted. And it will grow and become hard and heavy and will eventually lean out over the river. In time the tree cutters will cut down the tree and the wood carver will carve his digging tool and bury it in the mud of the living river to become as hard and as heavy as stone. And when this digging tool has been unearthed and left to sit for three planting seasons and given in the same way and with the same prayer to the nighttime digger of holes the hole digger himself will go with this tool to the place by the river where the knot maker has driven a stake. And here he will dig the hole that the knot maker has requested. Into this hole the knot maker will place his kwa seed, and the seed will grow, and when the kwa plant has taken full shape the knot maker will harvest its fibers in the way that knot makers do; in time he will roll the fibers into thread and the threads into strands and the strands into the rope that is used to make knots.

And now at last he will be ready to tie the knot that will give the storytellers the rope they need to spin wood into wood so they can make their fire—the very fire that the wood carver needs so he can find the lost digging tool for the hole digger to dig the hole that the adze maker needs to bury his blood so the wood carver can get his wood and the hole digger his tool and the knot maker his hole for the storyteller to make his fire. Carefully the knot maker will begin to tie the knot that will bind it all together.

And as the elderly knot maker steps forward the old woman's sons and daughters will follow without watching as he takes the two ends of the funeral rope. And the midwives will avert their eyes to the knot that will finally be tied and that will allow this unborn child to move from the other world to this one. And the fishermen will wait for their net. And the adze maker will await his adze. And the tree cutters will stand with their tree cutting tools raised high over their heads eyeing the hard neck of the leaning umbilical tree and waiting for the exact moment when the knot maker has finished this knot so that their cutting can begin.

By now the elderly knot maker has stepped forward. And while the seeing man is scattering a final fistful of salt on the ground to commemorate this knot the knot maker will give thanks for the knot that will be tied. And for the rain that has fallen. And the kwa that has grown. And the waters that are now flowing swiftly and strongly to connect the generations. And for the latest journey of this old woman from one life to another.

*It is a good hole that has been dug*, the knot maker will say as he takes up the ends of his rope, *And has certainly been worth the digging.*

And then he ties the knot.

ଊ   ଊ   ଊ

# FIRE

CR

N ow the hole can be dug. So the fibers can be planted. So the rope can be made and the smoke seen and the story told. For this is how the Old People make their fires: first, they tie a knot. To tie a knot they need a hole. And to dig their hole they first need the story of fire to be told. And so it is to the rhythmic sound of rope and stick—of one piece of wood being spun into another—that the Old People will tell their story of first fire.

*Long long ago*, they will begin, *there once was a knot that needed tying...*

CR

This was in the very beginning, before fire, when the only thing was silence. And this silence was so silent that no thing could come forth. No rope, only darkness. No digging, only night. This was the generation of deepest darkness when the silence slowly turned to darkness and the darkness turned slowly to night. From the silence came the darkness and from the darkness came the night. And this night was so dark that there was no thing to stir, only quiet. These were the generations of silence and darkness and night and quiet.

From this darkest of nights there came the earth out of the brine that covered all things. And this earth was covered in deepest darkness. And it was covered in brine until the earth came up from the brine and became the earth of the world. This was the generation of the briny ocean that covers the earth and the generation of the earth coming up through the brine to become the earth of all things. From the brine came the slime and from the slime came the mud. These were the generations of earth and brine and slime and mud.

Then from the mud that covered the earth there came the stones of the world. These were the hard stones that gave substance to the ground. And in the sky there came the movement of air that is the wind. The wind carried the air from one place to another until there was movement over the earth. The ocean began to stir. And across the cold stones of the island came the wind that carried the first seed of man into the mud.

And this mud was mud like any mud. Except that it was warm and fertile and into this mud there came from the wind a seed that fell deep into the mud and was buried there for forty generations. In the warmth of this darkness the seed lay buried in the mud through the forty generations of the world. And the generations were silence, darkness, night, quiet, earth, brine, slime, mud, stone, caves, wind, wonder, shadow, stars, clouds, moon, soil, rain, rivers, holes, pebbles, fiber, rope, wood, words, knots, adzes, stakes, digging, dawn, heat, day, sun, salt, prayer, smoke, indirectness, fire, silence, storytelling.

And when these generations had come to pass the mud shifted and the island's first knot maker awoke from the mud. And he saw nothing but night. And he felt nothing but silence and darkness and the cold wind that blew through the night. In the darkness of darkest night the knot maker traveled through the generations of his ancestors: through the mud and slime and the briny waters that were still covering the lower places of the earth. In darkness he made his way slowly through a world without rope—from brine to slime to mud—taking each unknown step in the cold slime and the churning brine and the mud. And as he traveled through the generations across the lower places of the island he felt a dull discord in his heart that told him that there could be nothing more to a knotless world than mud and slime and brine. For when he took the brine into his hands it could not stay in its place and fell without purpose through his fingers. And when he took the mud it refused to take a form.

And when he took up the slime in his hands it too took no shape. In this way the knot maker came to feel that the world itself was a soft thing for all he knew was the mud and slime and brine of the lower earth where he traveled. And the dull discord told him that the soft things would always be soft and that they would always fall where they fell; and that even the hard things of the world could not be made into knots for they would be hard in their own way and in their own way only.

But here a voice from within came to the knot maker and it told him that there was indeed more to the world than the soft things only and that there must be more than shifting wind and soft mud to give a girth to his knot making. For surely there must be more to the world than untold darkness and the shapeless feel of silence—and there must be more from which to make a rope than soft wind and shifting mud alone. And when this most primal of voices had come to him the knot maker resolved to find the things that could be taken together to give a higher rigor to his world.

And so the knot maker felt his way through a world without knots looking for a thing that could be tied. But the only things he felt were the mud and the brine and the slime and these did not have shape. And he felt the wind and the cold against his face and these too did not bring order. And the mud was soft and took no pattern;

the brine was cold and could not stay; and the slime was slick and gave no legacy. At this the knot maker became still at the formlessness of his quest. On an island that was quiet and dark he could not tell one end from the other; and in a world of many things he could not know which were simple and which were sacred—which of these things would not merely come and go, but would stay and stay forever. Once again the voice from within came to the knot maker and it told him that there truly could be a higher essence to his knot making and that it could be found in the spiraling rhythm that comes from the twisting of fibers into strands and strands into rope—and in the tying of rope into knots. And so it was during this longest and darkest of nights—the first night of the earth—that the knot maker began his quest for a thing to give texture and pattern to his world: for a rope that could be made out of the frayed fibers of silence and tied into a knot that might never be untied.

For many generations the knot maker traveled over the lower earth in search of a rope for his knot. In the darkest brine and the coldest mud he traveled until he came upon the firmness of stone in front of him. Here he reached out his hand to feel this stone and it was like nothing he had felt before. With no light to be seen he touched this hard thing and felt its firmness. And when he came upon another he did the same, feeling his way past it until he had gone from the lower earth where the brine and mud and slime still prevailed to the higher places where the stone of the ground was convincing and the caves were quiet and dark. To shelter himself from the wind the knot maker crawled deep inside these caves to where the darkness stays and the cold wind cannot come. And here he took shelter in the dry darkness of the caves.

In the caves there was nothing but darkness and the cool windless night. Within these caves the knot maker came to know the rough feel of the stone around him. And he felt his way along the endless passageways that led him from the opening in the mountain deeper and deeper into the darkness of the caves. Here he spent the quiet night at rest on the stone slab that lay in the furthest part of the deepest cave. And from here he came to know the passageways that led him back out from the depths of the earth to that same opening in the mountain where the caves ended and the world began. Yet when he came out of the darkness of the caves he felt nothing but the darkness of the world and the cold wind against his face.

And it was during this breathless time that the knot maker came to see that there must be more to the world than darkness and night alone. From burning darkness the knot maker felt a voice from afar and it told him that there must be light to see and that there must be a way for him to see it. For how can there be darkness without day? Or night without knowledge? Or silence without the sound of a fire burning outright? Yet in the shelter of his caves there could be nothing but deepest darkness and everlasting night. And in the darkness of first night there could be no light to be seen. And so it was that the knot maker, while searching for a rope for his knots, also began his search for the fire that would bring light to his eyes. This was in the early beginning when the earth was still quiet and dark and very far from fire. For fire itself could not come from the earth or the slime or the brine. And the darkness was undying. The wind was cold. And the caves gave shelter but no light.

Heavily the knot maker made his way from the silence of the caves through the darkness of the world looking for the fire that could make him see. Through the brine and the mud and the slime. Into the wind. Stumbling against first stone. From one silent place to another the knot maker carried his way through a world unseen with nothing to guide him but the voice that comes from within and a voice coming to him from afar. For there is light to be seen, he told himself. And at its heart there must be a fire to be made. And the cold wind blew. The silence prevailed. And the darkness of night grew darker. These were the generations of stone and caves when silence and darkness stood heavy on the earth and the wind blew cold through the night.

In the quiet of his own thoughts the knot maker grew weary from his search. With only the rough feel of the world to guide him he could not begin to make rope for his knots or knots for his fire. Nor could he know where fire itself was to be found. Without the comfort of seeing he walked across the barren night searching for the fibers to make his rope and the fire that would bring the light. From the caves he would set out. And to the caves he would return. With no fire. With no fibers. With nothing but the cold wind in his eyes and the dull glow in his heart. And even as the ocean subsided and the stones appeared and the earth began to take its form the knot maker could not see any of these things for his world was still among the original darkness that comes from the depths of deepest silence.

And it was at this very time in the dark world of shifting shapes and churning darkness that the knot maker searching for rope and fire felt in his heart a deeper emptiness that he could not explain. For in the silence of the world he listened but heard nothing. The world and its darkness were all along the crust of the earth and this crust went from one end of the world to the other; but it was shallow and barren and cold. Below it all, he thought, there must be a greater warmth to be felt—for the earth must surely be more than the things that are on its surface. Yet when he stood on the ground he felt nothing but the cold crust below. And it was hollow and brittle and unchallenged. If this is the extent of the earth, he thought, then it will forever be cold and shallow. The shallow and cold things will prevail. And these will become the things of the world. And so the knot maker searching for rope and fire also set out on a quest to find a thing that could upturn the earth and uncover the layers contained within: with neither tool nor promise nor precedent, the knot maker set out on his quest to find the secrets of hole digging and to dig the island's first hole.

And so it was in this way and during this time of great darkness and silence that the first seed of man came from the mud and stirred and was scattered upon the world; and it was in this way that the first rope would one day come to be made, the first hole dug, and the first story told. For these were the generations of wind and wonder, when the knot maker left the repose of warm mud in search of a hole for his rope, a rope for his fire, and a flame worthy of a hole that had never before been dug.

*Long long ago*, the Old People would come to say about this dark time, *there was a knot that needed tying.*

And it was during this time—during the tall part of the night while he was searching for fire and rope and the secrets of hole digging—that the knot maker stepped out from the opening of his cave to see a shadow: his own. This was the first thing that was ever seen by any man and it was seen by the knot maker at night when the stars had risen in the sky and were casting their dim light on the earth. In the distance he could hear the movement of fish in the ocean and it seemed that the silence too had finally given way around him. Above him was moon and on every side of him the shadows of the things that in his darkness had only been roughly felt: the stones and the mud and the opening in the mountain where the caves ended and the world began. Standing above first shadow, the knot maker looked around him to see the gloom that was now carrying itself over the earth. And in the pall of this dim light he saw a seed resting on the crust of the dry ground. The seed had been scattered by the wind in the night but had not been carried into mud. And now under the gloom from the moon and the stars the knot maker could see the seed shuddering in the cold. Was this the flame that he had been seeking?

Was this the secret to making rope for a knot that can be tied? For surely even the most patterned rope must come from those very things that do not have their own cadence? Surely the seeds of order must come from the deep mud of darkness? Carefully the knot maker took up the seed and held it in his hand and carried it with him as he made his way along the crusted earth.

Now the knot maker searching for a place for his seed could begin to take dim notice of the higher things in his world: of the clouds passing thinly in front of the moon; and the many stars in the sky; and the moon itself bringing shadow to the earth. Here the shapes of the clouds, ever thicker, could be seen moving across the sky. Looking at all of these far away things the knot maker could only wonder why they were moving in this way and not another. And whether there was a pattern to the stars and a purpose to the clouds and a consequence to the other things that he could now see. In the faint light from the moon he wondered which of these high things were truly high and which were only as high as they seemed. And in his heart he wondered whether these were really the higher things at all—the things that do not come and go but that stay in one place to the end, faithfully and forever.

And it was during this same time of gloom that the knot maker searching for a way to dig his hole looked down to see the other things that were in his world: the brittle ground underfoot where the mud had dried and turned to crust; and the shifting shadows made by the moon and stars; and the sudden rippling of the waters caused by the fish now moving from one place to another. In the barren light the knot maker noted the dim world around him from which no digging tool could possibly grow. For neither shadow nor stars nor the dark light from the moon could help him dig his hole. And the fish moving through the ocean were distant and unfathomable. And the stone was hard but cold; the wind was unknowable; and the brine and slime and mud—once prolific—were retreating to the farther places of the earth. To make his fire the knot maker would need more than gloom alone. To make his rope he would need more than the voice that comes from within. And to dig a hole that has never before been dug he would need more than a voice that comes quietly from afar. Making his way from one end of the world to the other the knot maker followed the vague and shifting shadows that he hoped would lead him to the unmarked places for hole digging. And as he looked up in wonder at the thickening clouds now gathering in the sky he saw that the island was becoming dark again. This was the time of first gloom when there was neither utter darkness nor utter day, during the generations of shadow and stars and clouds and moon.

Now the knot maker heard the clap of thunder and felt the rains come down from the clouds and listened as the rivers of the island began to stir. This was the time of the many flowing rivers. And these rivers came from the top of the mountain and brought the waters to the different places of the island. The knot maker knew these things because in the murky night he could see their faint waters and hear the crash of rain and the rush of the rivers and feel the mud soft and cold where they flooded. The waters came down from the mountain and became the many rivers that flow from the original river of the world. Yet during this time of rain coming down and rivers flowing there still was no fire to be found. For there were no holes. The pebbles that had descended from their stony ancestors had not been planted. And the fibers of the island, still struggling in the gloom, could not begin their journey from one life to another.

From the sound of the rain and the flow of the rivers the knot maker came to see that fire comes readily to no man and that the flame he was seeking could not come by his own efforts alone—but would instead come in its own time over the course of many generations. And so when he came to the place by the river where the rain had just come and when he saw the dim shape of a hole that had been formed by the weight of the waters—the first hole of the world—he placed his seed into the hole and sat himself next to it to wait.

Sitting by this seed the knot maker came to realize how far from fire he had become: that the fire he was seeking would not come at all without the rubbing of one stick into another, but that in order for the sticks to find their heat he would first need a rope that was quiet enough to spin them. Yet even this understanding—as hot and as true as it was—brought him no closer to fire itself. For no rope had ever been made or seen in the world: no fibers had ever been rolled into threads; no threads twisted into strands; and no strands made into a rope for a knot maker's knot. Sitting next to the umbilical seed now beginning to emerge from the ground next to him the knot maker gave thought to the rope that was needed for his knot making and to what a rope like this might look like. From this he came to foresee that a rope should be as long and as strong as its purpose, that it should be as firm and as faithful as rain, and that a rope of this kind could in fact be made from the fibers of the humble plant now growing faintly by the river. These were the days of the weaker light when the kwa plant struggled to give its fibers and the knot maker searching for fire struggled to see them.

In the lessening darkness around him the knot maker wandered the length of the many flowing rivers in search of the plant whose fibers were strong enough for rope yet humble enough to be taken. And when he came upon the kwa plant growing faintly along the river the knot maker knew to pay first homage to it—to the weakest of plants with the thinnest of bark, to the bleeding plant with its flesh and marrow and sinew. For the first time he took up the fibers and peeled the long strips from one end to the other—from where the quiet of the fibers ended to where their darkness began—and with these fibers in hand he returned to the tiny umbilical tree that was now emerging. In the gloom of night he sat beside the tree and as he sat he waited in silence for the secrets of knot making to come. Through the generations of holes and pebbles he waited with his frayed fibers under the growing umbilical tree—with nothing to guide him in the ways of knot making but the voice that comes from within and the voice that comes faintly from afar. And as he sat he wondered whether these voices would ever be fibrous enough for his knot making. Or whether they would continue to sit frayed and forlorn like the peeled fibers of his kwa. Under the darkness of the world's original umbilical tree the knot maker sat with his fibers; and in the darkness of the deepest caves he lay in sleep, his eyes still closed but his thoughts upturned.

And as he slept on his stone slab in the darkest and deepest part of the cave it happened that a different kind of voice came suddenly to the knot maker: the voice that comes from beyond. With his eyes closed he saw its light and in the glow of this light he came to see for the first time how the humble fibers could be made into the threads that become strands and the strands that become rope and the rope that can be used to make knots. In this way the knot maker travelled the long journey from fiber to rope, from deep within the narrowest passageways of original darkness where the voices meet and the fibers of the world are joined. So it was that the original knot maker came to understand the seeing that happens only in the utter darkness of the caves, where no light comes and no eyes see. The light that comes from beyond the opening in the mountain where the world ends and the caves begin.

Now sitting under the mature umbilical tree the knot maker took up the frayed fibers of first night and with the vision from the caves he made them into the threads that become strands and the strands that become rope and the rope that can be used to make knots. This was the first rope ever made and it was made by the knot maker under the umbilical tree that would become the island's original knotmaking tree. Yet when he had finally made this rope and could hold it in his hands—and it was as long and as strong as any purpose—the tired knot maker nevertheless understood that it would be no good at all without a knot to tie it off—for the fibers of the untied rope would soon unwind, and each time this happened his thoughts of knot making would quickly die back down to fiber. And so it was this unfinished rope—a rope that has not been tied—that the knot maker took and coiled over his shoulder in no particular direction and carried with him on his search for the knot to make his fire.

*It is a very good rope*, said the knot maker speaking words for the first time.

*But it comes undone*, came an unexpected answer.

*Do you think the humble plant can grow?*

*The moon and clouds are here.*

*There will be many ropes to make.*

*And many more knots to tie.*

*But what if the smoke does not come?*

*It is not easy to make fire from silence.*


And still no fire came to the knot maker. For even when the fiber had been made into rope and the wood for fire making had been found—and even when the first words for his world had come to be spoken—the knot maker could not make a fire to give the light. Each time the knot maker put his thoughts toward fire—each time he took out his rope to make a flame—he would see once again that the fibers of his rope had come undone and that the fire he was seeking would not come. With no knot there could be no rope. With no rope there could be no flame. And without a flame there could be no fire, no silence, no digging.

Only here when it seemed that it might not be a good thing for a man to have the light of fire—or even to search for it—did the knot maker come to understand the many things that must first happen for even the simplest fire to be made: that before you can have fire you must have the sticks that can be spun into each other; but that before you have the sticks you must have the wood. To get wood you must have a hole. And to dig a hole you must have the tool, the adze, the wood, the word. Here the knot maker came to understand the ancestry of fire and that this ancestry was in all things and must always be remembered. And so he traced his own path back through the generations that had come before: from shadow to wonder to wind. From caves to stone to mud. From mud to slime to brine to earth to quiet to night to darkness. And from this darkness all the way back to the very beginnings of silence.

In silence the knot maker sat alone in the growing gloom with his unborn rope and listened to the many sounds that must come before knot making: to the rush of the rivers now flowing and the crash of the ocean onto the beaches; to the silent rustle of the kwa in the night; and the dark sound of wind carrying the seeds of knot making into the mud. With no words to hear, the knot maker could only listen to the unspoken language of the ancient descendants of silence: the mud and the clouds and the stars and the stones and the moon and the soil and the rain.

And so it was during this generation of untied rope that the world's first knot maker sat in the gloom under the umbilical tree and devoted himself to discovering the secrets of knot making—to studying the first turns of this art. In the dim light of the stars he opened his heart to the ways of the knot and from this the knot maker came to see how a rope might become much more than the simple gathering of its fibers; that it can become something greater if it is pulled into itself and through itself and around itself; and that with the right intent it can become much more even than this—for this is what makes a knot a knot. Here he learned that the more turns in a rope the more likely there is to be a knot; and that the more turns in the knot the less likely the knot will be to slip, though the more likely to break. Gradually he came to know which end of a rope is its quiet end and which end carries the darkness; and from this he came to understand not just the great difference between the dark end of a rope and its quiet end but also the sacred union that takes place when the two are crossed. And when all of this had come to him like sudden light, he also came to see, out of the corners of his eyes, that a knot tied with a purpose is not just a function of the world but its fate: that a rope may be tied with either its dark end or its quiet end; but that the quiet end leads to knots that are quiet while the dark end leads to nothing but darkness.

In this way the knot maker sitting under the spreading umbilical tree began to reveal the secrets of knot making. For this was the generation of unmade knots when the knotmaking tree was born and the knot maker came to sit under it with his unfinished rope and his first thoughts of tying a knot that would never be untied.

But what the knot maker did not know as he searched among gloom for the knot to make his fire was that the many seeds of the island had already begun to wake from the mud where they too had been carried and that these seeds were now scattering themselves to the different places of the island: the island's first salt maker to the edge of the ocean where the salt crystals would one day form; the island's first seeing man to the ancient place where seeing has its navel; and the island's first midwife, her hands strong and ready, to the lower earth where the mud is fertile and the slime prevalent. Here the tree cutters grew from the mud. And the women of the island came forth. And the men who would make their living as fishermen with their first thoughts of taking fish. And the people of the quarry with their many stone ancestors. And the island's first storytellers with their stories of carried seed:

*Born was the island's first midwife and she was inexperienced.*

*Born was the first wood carver with no wood to carve.*

*Born was the tree cutter when there were no trees.*

*Born was the adze maker without an adze.*

*Born was the woman of first water.*

*Born were the people of the salt.*

*Born were the descendants of the quarry.*

*Born was the seeing man with nothing to see.*

*Born was the knot maker to a world without rigor.*

*Born was the storyteller in the days of wordless silence.*

*Born was the hole digger to the darkness of endless night.*

*Born were the people who live forever, the Old People.*

And so came the generation of the adze when the seed for the very first adze maker was carried by the wind into the mud. And then came the generation of the stake when the seed for the island's first wood carver awoke from this mud. And then came the generation of the digging that is done in darkness when the seed for the very first digging tool was placed into fertile mud to be found in forty generations. In time the wood carver carved his wood. The adze maker made his adze. And the digger of holes came to dig his first hole in the darkness of darkest night when the clouds were thick and the mud was thick and the night was dark enough for digging. In this way the wind brought the seed and the seed brought the rope. The rope brought the adze, the adze brought the stake, and the stake brought the digging that is done in darkness—the digging that can only be done in darkness.

And so the first digging was done. And it was in this way—during the generations of waning darkness—that the digging brought the dawn.

Looking up from his knot the knot maker could begin to see the soft glow of sky in the distance. This was new and as he looked toward the horizon he could see the lower stars going dimmer against the new light until they had faded into the sky—and then too the stars that were higher had faded: for the first time the sky was taking on the many shades of coming day. At this the knot maker grew fearful, for the stars had been his only light—each of them its own fire— and they were now leaving. The moon was going down. The sky was becoming unthinkable.

Now the glow grew brighter and as the light came from the back of the horizon it reached up to the top of the sky, higher and higher, until the stars had gone away completely and the sky itself had become smooth. At this the knot maker grew dim, for the stars had been his only promise of fire and they were now gone; around him the things of his world were taking on new light: the shapes gained dimension and the forms gained texture and degree. The hues of his existence grew subtle as the light from the dawn slowly revealed the world around him. The plants that were mere shapes in the gloom now had depth. And their colors were varied and gradual. And the knotmaking tree, the island's original umbilical tree, now had more shades of color in one leaf than the old knot maker had seen during his entire time on earth. This was the beginning, he knew, of a new era of subtle things: of lingering light and allusion. This was the generation of first dawn. And its descendants would be heat and day and sun.

And so the heat came and it settled over the land. And the first day came soon after. And the sun rose over the darkness. These were the generations of heat and day and sun. The knot maker watched all of this and as he saw these new things coming forth he knew that the old things would no longer be what they were. That the new things had come to the world and would stay and that the old things would be smaller throughout the earth. Here the voices told him that it was the sun and the day and their hot descendants that would claim the earth from the night. And that the long night—the one he had known and loved yet never truly seen—would itself be different. That there could be no other way.

After so many generations in the world the knot maker was now old; and after so much time spent in darkness his eyes were unready for the day. Looking at this new thing directly—after the darkness of such a long night—the knot maker felt his vision being overwhelmed, growing dim, and felt the generations going away from him once again: from light to shadow and back to darkness. Here the voice from within came together with the voice from afar to tell him that this light was not to be looked at directly; that he should look instead to the many other things in the world that are not sun. And yet it was all so new and so wondrous. The harsh glare of light in the sky. The warm rays of day. The hot heat digging into his dark eyes like stake into earth. All of it was so beautiful and new that he could do nothing but stare at it in wonder.

And the sun bore into his eyes with more brilliance than all the stars in the sky. And in this moment he came to see the sun and the sun only until everything else was lost. The light of all lights came into his eyes so deeply that he could see nothing at all. For this was the other side of seeing.

And the stars that had shone above him during his long night now came to him in their opposite: as black stars that shimmered and moved against the hot light. And the light was his darkness, and the swirling points of darkness his light. Fire is a beautiful thing indeed, he thought, and will certainly be worthy of the darkness. The fire came into his eyes. And the day shone upon him. The heat came hot. And it seemed that this new light would last forever. And as he sat in the bright shade of the umbilical tree he gazed tenderly into the sun that had now become his eyes. The day stood tall. The heat warmed. And the sun gave the light that it gives.

*Fire really has been worth the darkness*, he said using words that had never before been spoken. *For it is bright and new and necessary.*

And this fire truly was new, with a burning glare that left no room for any other. With a brightness so hot that nothing more would ever need to be felt—neither heat, nor flame, nor light. From this day forward, he knew, no other thing would ever be needed beyond the heat and warmth and relentless glare of this new hot light.

Silently the knot maker turned away. From the sun. From the day. From the light that had finally come to the earth. From the new things. For it was at this moment that he came to see with his full vision what it means to look at a thing directly. And that there are things that have light that should not be seen. And things that should be seen but never looked at. Achingly he understood that there are things that should not be overlooked while they are still in the world to be seen. For even the night—as long and as deep as it is—cannot outlive the day. And so he turned away. And as he closed his eyes the new light faded to darkness. The black stars faded once again beyond the horizon of his vision.

*Fire is a great thing indeed*, he thought, *but it too must slowly burn down to ash.*

In the ancestry of knot making, these were the generations of utter day—of sun and heat—when the island's oldest knot maker looked directly at the light, then turned away forever.

And what the knot maker now saw with his eyes forever closed was the long path that he had traveled. The generations of knot making leading from one silence to the other, from darkness through shadow to light. These were the ancestors that had dried the brine and scattered the seed and given the fertile shelter of warm mud. These were the caves and the stars and the moon and the clouds and the soil and the rain and the holes. These were the rivers that flowed from the womb of the earth and gave life to all living things. These were the heat and the day and the sun that had been sent to gouge out his eyes. Looking back, it all came together at once.

With the sun now seen and with only his knot left to tie, the knot maker gathered the things that he had been carrying for so long—his coil of unfinished rope, the fire sticks that had never known fire, his unplanted pebbles and simple salt—and headed back toward the dark shelter of his caves. And as he walked for the final time the knot maker passed the things of the island that he had not seen and could not now see: the blue ocean and the orange mountains and the golden river sparkling under the sun as it connected them to each other. In the new light of day he passed the many trees of the island that now grew in so many shades of green that they could not be named; and the brightly colored fish moving through the sea; and the blinding white of the salt that was already starting to form in drying pools under the hot sun. In the new darkness of his mind he saw without seeing that the mud was deep and brown and the passing clouds were silver and that his hands had become a dark color of red from the long night spent with his fibers. He saw all of this with eyes that could no longer see.

And with eyes that could not yet see he saw the many generations of the world now spreading out across the island. The people of the quarry looking in wonder at the stones that lay before them. The adze maker trying to make an adze that has never before been made. The island's first midwife standing over the womb of the world's original mother. And the wood carver with his wood. And the storyteller with his smoke. And the hole digger with his tool. All of this came to the breathless knot maker as he made his way back to the cool and familiar darkness where one story ends and another begins.

The cave by now was as old as the wind—more vast and more ancient than the sun—and when the knot maker reached the opening in the mountain where the light ends and the darkness begins he went inside, going with his things deeper and deeper until he had reached the place where no wind can go and no day can come. This was the place of his stone slab. Here, at last, he sat himself down on the heavy slab of stone; and taking the things that he had brought—the wooden sticks and the pebbles and the coil of unfinished rope now ready for its sacred ending—the knot maker began to tie his knot.

In familiar darkness the eldest of all knot makers sat with the things that he had spent so long coming to know—the sticks and pebbles and rope and salt—and here, in the darkness, he said his first prayer. For the making of this knot: that it was not being tied improperly or before its time; and that it would only be used for the most sacred of purposes: to tie up an unfinished rope; to make a knot that will never be unmade; to celebrate the passing from one life to the next. Here the knot maker prayed for the long life of the knot: that it would not slip or break or come undone during the hottest moments of fire making when the stick begins to spin; or the hurried moments of tree cutting when the tree begins to fall; or the perilous moments of the windy months when the womb begins to rattle. And that when this knot had been made and left in the depths of the caves that there would forever be people to find it— new people—and that they would not overlook it, or turn away from it, or be blinded by the dark feeling that comes after a fire has died down and it is time to turn away from the warm darkness of light and to head toward the cold darkness of silence. Here he took the residue of first salt and rubbed it into his earthly skin and tasted this salt and praised it and spread it over the ground. Finishing his prayer the knot maker waited for the light that only he can see: the dying glow of ember that would tell him that it was time to tie his knot—and that the moment for this tying had finally come.

And when he had at last seen these things the knot maker knew with all the voices in his heart that the time for his knot had indeed come; and that he would be able to tie it; and that it would be a knot that was worth the tying. Here he took up the rope now made and with one hand holding the quiet end and the other hand holding its dark end, and with a final prayer for the tying to be done, the knot maker tied the knot.

And all the while the trees of the island rejoice in the new warmth. The sun has finally risen and now hangs above the place by the ocean where the brine gathers under the sun to become salt. The air is warm and in the light that can only come after hole digging the clouds move across the blue sky. The warm wind of the island blows one way then the other. The earth becomes the heat. The plants begin to grow and an umbilical sapling emerges. At last the sun begins to descend over the place near the beach where the brine has turned to salt under the sun. The nighttime rains pool in the mountains and come down through the rivers to the place by the beach where the simple salt turns sacred. The clouds grow thicker and move ever more thickly across the sky. The winds blow harder. The rain falls and the rivers flow. In time the generations pass from one to the other like a sigh through the caves. The kwa plant grows slowly and humbly and finally takes its form. The first fire is made. The wind scatters it all to ash and the seed of the island's original salt maker is carried into the salt beds to lie buried. In the cool and quiet darkness of the caves the first knot of ancestry and descent will be found in forty generations. Now, in the long silence that comes after fire making, the storyteller can add his words.

CR

This is how the Old People tell their stories: first, they tie a knot.

And so when the fire of the village has died down to ash, the ancient storyteller will resume the story of first fire by telling how the island's eldest knot maker stepped forward to tie his knot. And how this knot would one day be used to hold a roof to itself; and to guide a falling tree to the ground; and to bring an unborn child from the other world to this one—and then, much later, to send her back again. Here the storyteller will tell of the first knot ever made and how it was tied by the island's first knot maker in the depths of the deepest caves and how, after he had tied the knot, the knot maker then wrapped this first rope around his waist—from one end to the other—and tied it off at the navel; and how the very old knot maker then lay back on his stone slab to wait for the embers of his fire to burn down; and that this was how the knot maker had left the very first knot of ancestry and descent to be found in the caves.

Here the storyteller will tell of the knots that came from this first knot and of all the knots that have then come from these knots in turn. And in this way the storyteller will tell the story of every rope made, of every knot tied. Faithfully, he will tell of the adzes carved and the fish caught and the waters carried. He will tell of the old tree cutter who once fell from a high place while doing his cutting but who now stands near the leaning umbilical tree with his cutting tool held high over his head. And he will tell of this very old tree that has been waiting to fall for many generations and that in a few short moments will be felled for the sake of the Old People's prayer. The storyteller will tell all these things—and by so doing he will give to his world the story of the winds that shift and the mud that stays and the water that flows and will always flow.

*It is a very long river*, the storyteller will say, *and its waters are sure to last forever.*

At this the Old People will be averting their eyes to the story being told and listening in wordless silence. Countless generations of knot making have taught them that it is not a good thing to look too closely at a story being told—and that silence must always be respected. For only silence has no ancestor.

And the wind will blow. And the trees will rustle. And the smoke will rise from the first fire made and, from the depths of the caves, blow in many directions at once. Soon the hungry sand crab will be coming up from his hole.

And when this story too has burnt down to ash the Old People will pick up the things of their day and head back to their houses.

*It has been a very good fire to have made*, the Old People will remember. *And a knot that has been worth the making.*

For now the holes of the island are dug. Now the fire of this day can be put out. Now the story of silence has been told.

And now the knot is tied.

ଘ   ଘ   ଘ